MOUNTAIN JACK PIKE

FIRE IN THE HOLE

#12

Also by Robert J. Randisi

MOUNTAIN JACK PIKE

FIRE IN THE HOLE

#12

Robert J. Randisi

SPEAKING VOLUMES, LLC
NAPLES, FLORIDA
2013

Fire in the Hole #12

ISBN 978-1-61232-603-0

CHAPTER ONE

Jack Pike and Skins McConnell were camped on Henry's Lake, and had been for several months. Their time was spent hunting, trapping; they had even done some fishing. They hadn't seen another soul for all that time, which was why it was so odd to see the smoke to the north.

"A campfire for sure, McConnell said.

"Yeah," Pike said, "but whose?"

Actually, they *had* seen some other souls, but those had been Indians—who probably didn't *have* souls. They hadn't seen any white men the whole time, but they felt that these campfires were from a white camp.

"What do you think?" McConnell asked.

"About what?"

"Are you curious enough to go and take a look?" McConnell asked.

Pike looked north at the smoke and said, "That's got to be better than twenty miles."

"So?"

5

"So," Pike said, with a shrug, "let's go and take a look."

Joe Gall looked over his camp and was dissatisfied with what he saw. They were a small party of maybe fifteen or so, camped on the Gallatin Fork, *exactly* twenty miles from Pike's camp on the lake.

Gall rarely led parties of his own, and this one was an offshoot of a larger one. Gall usually did his work under Nathan Wynan, but had decided to go off on his own. He had managed to convince some of Wynan's other men to go with him, resulting in this small hunting party. Wynan's party consisted of forty or more men, even without these. Wynan's people had the ultimate confidence in him, and that's what Joe Gall was after.

This was Gall's camp, and he was proud of it. Sure, they had lost some men along the way to the many dangers the mountains presented. Some had even deserted and gone back to Wynan. And sure, they were running low on supplies, and blankets, and their animals were worn out, but this was *still* Gall's camp, and he wanted to try to keep it together as long as he could.

Unfortunately, there were still some more of Gall's men who were planning to leave. . . .

Of the men who were still in camp three in particular were planning to leave, and wanted others to come with them. They were Sam Healy, Tom Meggett and Steve Hobbs.

6

"Who else can we count on?" Healy asked. The three men were sitting around a campfire, away from the other men, making their plans to leave.

"I think we can count on Walters," Meggett said. "He's got a wife here with him. He'd like to get her back to the safety of Wynan's camp."

"So does Kincaid," Hobbs said.

Walters's and Kincaid's wives were the only women in camp—unless you counted Hobbs' Indian woman. She was Crow, and he called her "Woman," never addressing her by her name, which was Bright Deer. She cleaned for him, cooked for him, warmed his bed, and anyone else's *he* told her to warm on those rare occasions that he was drunk enough to share her with others. No one really liked Hobbs, but they admired the way he had his Indian squaw trained.

"That makes five of us," Healy said. "When the others see five of us—"

"Eight, with the three women," Hobbs said.

"Right, right, eight," Healy said. "When the others see the eight of us pullin' out, they're sure to want to come along."

Meggett moved his shoulders uncomfortably and said, "I feel kind of—ya know, disloyal."

"To who? Gall?" Healy asked. "What the hell for? Look what he's led us to. We stay out here any longer with him and we'll end up dead, our bones being picked by the Blackfeet, or the buzzards." He laughed shortly and said, "You want to stay, Meggett, be my guest, but I'm gettin' out of here while I still can. I made a mistake following Gall out of Wynan's camp, and I'm gonna correct that mistake as soon as I can."

7

"I didn't say I wanted to stay," Meggett said, quickly. "I'm just sayin' that Gall had, you know, good intentions and all—"

"Good intentions, bad intentions, Healy said, cutting him off sharply, "we're still gonna end up dead if we stay here with him. Make up your mind, Tom. Are you with us or not?"

"Hell, sure I'm with you, Sam, you know that," Meggett said.

"All right, then," Healy said, "all we got to do now is pick our time."

"Soon," Hobbs said, "let's make it soon, huh?"

"The sooner, the better," Healy agreed, privately adding, before somethin' else goes wrong. . . .

Joe Gall saw the three men with their heads huddled together and knew what it meant. They were talking about leaving, and if they did, some of the others would probably follow.

Gall figured he needed something, maybe a miracle, in order to keep his camp together. . . .

"Pike," McConnell said, "that smoke looks like it's coming from the valley."

"That's a bad place to camp," Pike said, shaking his head. "That's a goddamned natural trap if they get attacked."

"Should we tell them?" McConnell asked.

"Tell them that they're fools for camping there?" Pike asked. "How would you like some strangers to come riding into your camp to tell you that?"

"Well . . . not in those exact words," McConnell said, "but I wouldn't *make* a dumb move like that. Besides, we don't know that they *are* strangers until we reach their camp."

"I don't know anybody who would make a dumb move like that," Pike grumbled.

"Well," McConnell said, "let's keep going and take a better look."

They continued riding until they came within view of the camp.

"Jesus," McConnell said. "They're hardly up to beaver, are they?"

"Let's go down and talk to them," Pike said, and then added, *"just* talk."

"You mean you *ain't* gonna tell them what fools they are?"

"No man likes to be called a fool, Skins," Pike said, "but maybe we can tell them . . . without really *telling* them."

Not being "up to beaver" meant they were a poor looking lot. Pike and McConnell rode noisily into the valley, announcing their appearance so no one would mistake them for Indians. Anyone who was fool enough to camp in a valley would also be fool enough to shoot without looking first. The last thing Pike needed was to be killed by some damned fool.

As they rode into the camp they saw that the men were badly equipped for this. They seemed to be light on supplies, blankets, traps. Off to one side was a flimsy pole corral filled with rawboned mules and ringtailed horses. In every way possible the camp was ill-fitted to resist an Indian attack, should one come. Camped in a narrow valley, they were flanked by steep bluffs which were covered with trees, and the bottom of the valley was deep with brush and grass.

Pike and McConnell rode in and were welcomed heartily. They knew instinctively that the only reason they were welcomed so openly was because morale was so low. If men were poorly equipped, they were extremely hospitable.

The "booshway" in camp, they discovered, was a man named Joe Gall. Pike and McConnell didn't know him, but they knew Nathan Wynan.

"I was with Nathan for a long time," Gall said, "before I decided to strike out on my own."

Pike and McConnell both looked around and had to bite their tongues to keep from saying something about the poor appearance of the camp.

In the end Gall invited Pike and McConnell to share their food and spend the night in camp. Since it was too late in the day for them to ride back to their own camp before dark, they reluctantly accepted. After all, it would only be for one night.

What could go wrong?

Gall insisted that Pike and McConnell be seated at his fire. They ate with him, but then mixed in with the other men. That was when they learned of the hardships the party had gone through, and of the desertions they had experienced.

"To tell you the truth," one of the men confided to McConnell, "some of us are thinkin' about goin' back to Wynan, too."

"Nate Wynan?" McConnell said.

"Yeah," another man said. "Nate never let his camp go bad like this."

McConnell knew Wynan, and knew he was a good man. He was surprised, if Gall had learned from Wynan, that Gall ran such a shoddy camp.

"Tell the truth," the first man said. "You were shocked when you first rode in, right?"

"Well . . ." McConnell said.

"Don't lie," the other man, Sam Healy, said. He was fairly vocal in his criticism of Joe Gall's camp.

"Well . . ." McConnell said again.

"You don't want to say nothin'," the man said, "but you don't have to. I can see it in your face . . . and it ain't gonna get any better. I don't see where we have much choice."

McConnell couldn't help but agree, although he did not voice his agreement. Still, he felt dishonest in his silence. . . .

CHAPTER TWO

Pike took a walk through the camp. That's when he discovered that there were three women there. He would ask Gall about them later. Two of them were white, and one was an Indian. The white ones were in their late thirties or early forties, sturdy women, the kind trappers married. The Indian woman was in her twenties, and very pretty. The man she was with was older, and even while Pike saw them in passing, he could see that he treated her like a servant. That didn't necessarily mean they weren't married, though.

The Indian woman—she looked like Crow to Pike—saw him looking at her and caught his eyes, holding them boldly as he passed. She looked proud and strong. He wondered why she stayed with the man. Well, that wasn't really his business, was it?

Pike sat with Gall at his fire again, for coffee, and asked about the women.

"Kincaid and Walters are married. The Indian girl you saw belongs to Hobbs."

"They're not married?"

"No," Gall said. "Hobbs is a pig. I don't know any woman who would marry him. No, he owns her. He's got her well trained."

"Does he mistreat her?"

Gall looked at Pike and said, "I guess, but that's his business. I don't interfere."

"I see."

"I know it don't look like much," Gall said, looking around the camp, "but it's mine."

Pike didn't say anything. Like McConnell, though, it made him feel dishonest.

Gall looked across the fire at Pike, then shook his head and said, "Yeah, who am I kiddin', right? It's dyin'." He waved his arms and added, "I'm no Nathan Wynan, Pike. I don't know how to keep men together, I'm not an organizer. I thought I was."

"I heard talk that some of the men went back," Pike said.

"Yeah," Gall said, "and more probably want to go, too. Healy, Hobbs, Meggett, they think I don't know that they're plannin' to leave . . . and take others with them, no doubt."

Joe Gall was a tall, slender man with a heavy black beard shot with grey. He appeared to be in his early forties, and maybe he was just tired of being a follower his whole life. Just once he wanted to be a leader, and now he was finding out that he wasn't cut out for it.

13

"What about you?" Pike said.

"What about me?"

"Why don't you go back?" Pike said. "Wynan would probably take you back."

"I know he would," Gall said, "but that would be admittin' that I was a failure."

"Gall," Pike said, "if the others go back, you can't stay out here alone."

"I know, I know," Gall said. "If they decide to go back, *I'll* probably go with them."

Pike looked around at the steep bluffs and said, "You'd be well advised to move before the Blackfeet find you, Joe. This is a perfect place for an ambush."

"I know that," Gall said. "It's not an ideal place to camp, but everyone was so damned tired—the men, the animals—that we *had* to stop. We'll get movin' as soon as we're well rested enough."

"Well, Skins and I will head back to our own camp tomorrow," Pike said. "I wish you the best of luck with the rest of your time."

"Some of the men may ride a ways with you," Gall said. "We might as well raise our traps and see what we've got before we break camp."

"Good enough," Pike said.

"Good night, Pike," Gall said. "Maybe I just needed to hear from somebody else what a fool I've been bein'."

"You didn't need me to tell you anything, Joe," Pike said. "You would have made the right decision on your own. Good night."

Pike walked away from Gall's fire. He still felt

dishonest, but at least the man seemed to know how bad things were. Now all he had to do was the right thing.

Pike and McConnell had their own blankets, and spread them for a night's sleep.

"So?" McConnell said.

"So what?"

"Did you tell him?"

"Tell him what?" Pike asked.

"That he's a fool?"

"Didn't have to," Pike said, trying to get comfortable. "He already knew."

"Most of his men are ready to go back to Wynan's camp, McConnell said. "I talked to some of them."

"You talk to anyone named Hobbs? Or Healy?"

McConnell thought a moment, then nodded.

"Yeah, I talked to Healy," he said. "He seems to be the one urging the others to leave camp. Why?"

"Gall knows they're planning to leave."

"What's he gonna do about it?"

"He said he might even go with them."

"Smart man."

"You didn't meet Hobbs?"

McConnell shook his head.

"Why?"

"Hobbs apparently has an Indian woman—"

"I saw them," McConnell said, recalling. "She don't look happy."

"That's what I thought."

"You gonna rescue her?"

"I don't take other men's women, Skins," Pike said, giving his friend a look.

"There are a couple of married men here, with their wives," McConnell said. "I'd say they'd be about ready to leave."

"I agree."

"Gall would be real smart to go with them."

"If the others decide to do it," Pike said, "he'll go with them."

"That's good," McConnell said, looking around them into the dark. "To tell you the truth, I don't feel so great about being around here myself, even if it's just for the night."

"We'll get out at first light," Pike said.

"Or before," McConnell said.

Both men turned over and went to sleep.

Or tried to . . .

They rose just before first light, had some coffee and then saddled their horses. Five of the men from Gall's camp also saddled up. Gall stayed behind.

"I talked to some of my men last night," Gall told Pike.

"And?"

"We'll be headin' back to Wynan's camp before the day is out," Gall said. "Hopefully our traps will yield somethin', and we'll have somethin' to contribute when we go back."

"It's a good decision, Joe," Pike said.

"I know," Gall said, "and the best one I've made in a long time." Then he added, "Maybe the *only* good one I've made in a long time."

"It won't. be your last good one," Pike assured him, although he wasn't so sure. . . .

The seven men — Pike, McConnell and five of Gall's trappers, including the man Pike knew as Hobbs — rode out of the camp together and headed upriver. When they reached the point where the traps had been set Pike and McConnell stopped with them instead of continuing on.

The five men dismounted and waded out into the tributary to check their traps. Pike and McConnell remained mounted, and that was why they spotted the Blackfeet before the Indians were on them.

It was a party of about forty Indians, and they were coming fast. Their intent was obvious.

"Blackfeet!" Pike shouted. "Everybody out!"

It looked like Joe Gall hadn't made his good decision soon enough.

CHAPTER THREE

Both Pike and McConnell raised their rifles and fired at the charging Indians, but it did little to dissuade them. They just kept coming.

"Out! Out!" McConnell was shouting. He grabbed up the reins of three of the trapper's horses and rode out into the water with them. The other two horses had spooked and strayed too far for him to grab them.

Two trappers came running out of the water after their horses, but the animals were too spooked by the commotion and were not cooperating. Healy was one of the men.

The Indians had rifles and were firing them. One of the trappers cried out, spun around and went down. Pike thought he remembered the man's name as Meggett. The other, Healy, had his foot in his stirrup, but his horse wouldn't stand still. The animal finally reared, throwing the man to the ground, and then ran off.

In the water the three trappers whose horses

McConnell had brought them were mounted up. They grabbed up their rifles and fired at the Indians. One or two braves fell from their horses, but the others kept coming.

"Let's get out of here!" Pike shouted.

McConnell and the trappers in the water turned their horses and started riding back towards Gall's camp.

Pike wheeled his horse about and rode to the fallen Healy, who was getting to his feet. He extended his arm, and as the man reached up to grab it, his face was blown away. Pike actually had ahold of the man's arm, but he was holding nothing but dead weight. He released the body, and it fell to the ground. Pike turned his horse and rode after McConnell and the others.

It occurred to Pike that maybe they should be leading the Blackfeet *away* from Gall's camp, but the men ahead of him were in full flight, and there was no way he'd be able to stop them now.

They were going to find out just *how* ill-equipped Joe Gall's camp was to handle an Indian attack.

Gall's own men reached the camp first, shouting warnings to the others. McConnell rode in behind them, and Pike last.

Pike found Gall and shouted, "Get as many rifles as you have and be ready to fire!"

As it turned out there were about a dozen rifles in camp that were in working order, not counting Pike's and McConnell's. There weren't even enough firearms for each man, so two men had to be designated to load while the others fired. There was also a shortage of powder, so Pike gave instructions not to fire just for the sake of firing. He told them to make sure they had a target before they fired. Gall didn't seem to mind Pike's taking over and giving orders.

"What happened to Meggett and Healy?" Gall asked, looking around.

"They're dead," Pike said.

"Damn it—"

"And we'll all be dead unless we get ready—" Pike started, but there was no time to get ready, or for him to finish his statement.

The Blackfeet were on them.

Pike, McConnell, Gall and the others did their best. They fired, reloaded as fast as they could, and fired again. At least they slowed the Blackfeet down and kept them from riding right over the camp. Instead, the Indians dismounted and took to the bluffs for cover. That was when the situation Pike and McConnell had been afraid of came into being.

The trappers were caught in the small valley with Blackfeet in the bluffs around them. They were pinned down, with nowhere to go.

Foxholes were hastily dug, and the men and women hurried into them, but Pike had another idea. The Indians obviously wanted what the trappers had, especially their mules and horses.

"Skins, come on!" Pike shouted.

He and Skins were in the open, because there weren't enough foxholes.

"Where to?"

"The corral."

"There's no cover there."

"The horses will be the cover," Pike said. "They won't shoot the horses."

Pike, McConnell and one other man ran for the corral and threw themselves into the midst of the animals. The other man simply did not have a foxhole to scamper into, so he had followed Pike and McConnell.

And suddenly, as quickly as it had began, the shooting stopped, and it was quiet.

"You were right," McConnell said. "They've stopped firing."

"Yeah," Pike said, "for now."

The other man with them, Hobbs, said, "What are we supposed to do?"

"Figure out a way out of here," Pike said.

"How?" McConnell said. "They've got us pinned down from all sides."

"Yeah," Pike said, "but they won't rush us, not as long as they want these animals."

"Why would they want *these* animals?" McConnell asked no one in particular, looking around.

"How long will that last?" Hobbs asked, responding to Pike's comment.

"I don't know," Pike said. "Sooner or later they'll realize that they can just come and take whatever they can get."

"Maybe we ought to just make a run for it," McConnell said.

"I've got to talk to Gall and the others," Pike said. "If we're going to make a break, we've got to make it together, at the same time. That way at least *some* of us will have a chance to get away."

"We're in here with the horses now," Hobbs said. "Why don't we just mount up and get out?"

Pike looked at the man and saw the panic creeping into his eyes. It wasn't naked, uncontrollable panic yet, but it would soon be, and Pike was sure that others were feeling the same thing.

"There are women in camp, Hobbs," Pike said. "In fact, one of them is yours, if I'm not mistaken."

"She's just a squaw," Hobbs said. "I ain't about to die for her."

"You get on a horse now, and you're a dead man," Pike said.

"You said they wouldn't shoot at the horses!" Hobbs said.

"No, not the Blackfeet," Pike said. *"I'll* shoot you if you try to desert the others."

"What?" Hobbs stared at Pike, popeyed, not sure he had heard the man right at all.

"You heard me," Pike said. "We all leave at the same time, or not at all."

"That's crazy—"

"If you try to ride out now, alone, they'll just shoot you down, horse or no horse," McConnell said. "Don't you see? If we all ride out at the same time, and split up, some of us will have a chance of gettin' away."

"And the others?"

"The others will end up dead," Pike said.

"Oh yeah?" Hobbs said. "Well, who chooses who lives and who dies?"

Pike pointed up at the Blackfeet on the bluffs and said, "They do . . . right now, they're calling all the shots . . ."

Pike couldn't think of a way to get to Gall without getting shot at, so he finally decided to call out to the man.

"Gall!"

"I'm here."

"Anybody hurt?"

There was a few moments of silence during which Gall checked with his people.

"Don't seem like it," he finally called out. "What made them stop shooting?"

Pike lowered his voice, hoping that Gall would still be able to hear him, but that the Blackfeet wouldn't. He told Gall why they thought the Indians had stopped shooting for now, and what he and McConnell—and Hobbs—had been talking about.

"Don't be a fool, Pike," Gall said. "Get on those horses and get out of here. Stampede 'em. That'll give you cover."

"See?" Hobbs said. "I agree with him."

Pike and McConnell both ignored him.

"There's got to be another way," Pike said. "You and your men just sit tight in those holes. We'll think of something."

"We will?" McConnell asked.

"Yeah," Pike said. "Don't we always?"

"*I* always come up with the plans," McConnell said.

"You?"

"That's right."

"Oh, yeah, that's right," Pike said, "it was *your* idea to ride over here to see where the smoke was coming from, right? I got to give you credit for that."

"That wasn't a plan," McConnell said.

"No? What was it?"

There was a pause, and then McConnell said, "An agreement . . . yeah, that's what it was, an agreement. We both *agreed* to ride over here."

"It was your idea."

"Hell no, it was yours."

"If you two don't shut up," Hobbs said, "I'm gonna let the Indians shoot me just so I can get away from you."

"Take it easy," Pike said. "We're just trying to lighten up the mood."

"Yeah, see?" McConnell said to Hobbs. "Even *you* just made a joke."

Hobbs looked at McConnell from beneath a sway backed horse and said, "I wasn't jokin'."

Joe Gall wasn't in the mood for jokes, either.

Gall was looking up at the bluffs, wondering why he had ever thought that he could ever lead anyone. He wasn't feeling much like a leader, at the moment. Thank God Pike had taken charge when he did, or they might all be dead now. From here on in he'd let Pike make the decisions.

All Joe Gall was feeling now was panic. It was welling up from deep inside of him until he thought he would burst, but he was trying not to let it show. He had to make everyone believe that he was calm. At least he could do *that* much for the people who had followed him here.

Couldn't he?

As the day wore on there were some exchanges of shots back and forth, but neither side made any kind of significant move.

"Maybe they'll just get tired and leave," Hobbs said at one point.

"Not much chance of that," McConnell said.

"I agree," Pike said.

"Well, what if we let the animals out?" Hobbs suggested. "They would collect them, and then maybe they'd leave?"

"If we did that," McConnell said, "they'd have the animals, and then they'd ride down here and kill us all. Besides, they'd still want the women."

"So why don't we just give them what they want?" Hobbs said.

Both Pike and McConnell gave the man a look.

"Are you going to tell two men that they have to give up their wives to save your life, Hobbs?" Pike asked, his distaste for the man plain in his tone.

"Hell, I'll give up my squaw—"

"I don't think I want to hear anything else from you, Hobbs," Pike said.

"Well, I don't hear either of *you* comin' up with an idea," Hobbs said.

"We're thinkin'," McConnell said. He looked at Pike and said, "Ain't we?"

"I am," Pike said. "I thought you were asleep."

"More jokes?" Hobbs asked.

"No," McConnell said, "he's right. I dozed off."

Hobbs shook his head and looked away in disgust.

"What are we gonna do?" McConnell asked Pike in a low voice. "Those Blackfeet ain't gonna wait much longer. We've got to make a move before they do—before somebody decides to panic."

"I know it," Pike said. "I can feel the panic in the air."

McConnell nodded.

"So can I."

Suddenly, Pike sniffed at the air, and McConnell noticed.

"What?" McConnell asked, frowning and also smelling the air. "You can *smell* the panic?"

"Do you smell something . . ." Pike said.

McConnell lifted his head higher, as if that would help him catch the scent better.

26

"What?"

"Something . . . else?"

"Like what?"

This time, however, they both smelled it at the same time.

"Smoke?" McConnell said.

They stood up and looked over the backs of the horses and mules. Hobbs noticed.

"What's the matter?" he asked, standing up. "You guys see somethin'? Are they leavin'?"

"No," Pike said, "they're not leaving. Not by a long shot."

Up in the bluffs they could see the flare of fiery torches.

"Is that . . . fire?" Hobbs asked, his tone hushed . . . and frightened.

"Jesus," Pike said, in the same tone, "if they touch those torches to the grass down here . . ."

". . . we'll be caught in a sea of flames," McConnell finished for him.

CHAPTER FOUR

They had to do something fast.

"The others are bound to see those torches," Pike said. "They'll panic and spook for sure."

"What can we do about it?"

"You stay put!" Pike said.

"Wait—" McConnell started, but Pike had already left the cover of the corral and animals and was running back towards Gall and the others.

The shooting started again, and when Gall and his men saw Pike running their way they fired to give him cover, as did McConnell and Hobbs from the other side. By the time Pike reached them, everyone was reloading.

There was no room for Pike in anyone's fox-hole—especially since he was so big—so he just lay down flat on the ground next to Gall.

"What the hell are you trying to do, Pike, get yourself killed?" Gall asked.

"Fire," Pike said.

"What?"

"The Blackfeet are going to use fire."

Gall looked around them, then up into the bluffs. When he saw the torches, his mouth went dry.

"In this valley . . ." Gall said, letting it trail off. He obviously understood the situation.

"I know," Pike said.

"What do we do?" Gall asked.

"First of all you've got to keep your people from panicking," Pike said.

Gall looked at Pike with wide eyes.

"I don't know if I can do that, Pike," he said, his voice shaking. "Jesus, I don't even know if I can keep *myself* from panicking."

"You'll do it, Joe," Pike said. "A lot of lives depend on you."

Gall swallowed with difficulty and said, "A-all right. What else do we do?"

"We'll have to wait as long as we can and then make a break for it."

"That's what the Indians want, though," Gall said. "The fire is to force us into making a break."

"I know," Pike said. "We just won't make it when they're expecting it."

"Like now?"

Pike nodded.

"I think that's why they're not making any secret of what they're going to do. They're trying to panic us into moving before we're ready."

Indeed, some of the other men had already seen

the torches and knew what was going to happen. Pike could feel the panic in the air more than ever.

"Keep your men as calm as you can, Joe," he said. "Don't let them make a break until we—you and I—say so. Understand?"

"Totally," Joe Gall said. "The Blackfeet will expect us to try and get away *before* they start a fire in the grass, right?"

"Right. We're going to force them into doing it, and then the smoke will cover us all," Pike said. "They won't be able to see any better than we can. When we break, we'll all break at the same time. Some of us are bound to get away in the confusion."

"All right," Gall said. "I'll do my best to control the men."

"Good man," Pike said. "Give me some cover. I've got to get back to the corral. The animals are going to go crazy when they smell the flames. If we let them out, it'll add to the confusion."

"All right," he said, then raised his voice and called out, "let's make some noise!"

As Gall and his men started firing again, Pike ran back to the corral and slid underneath it.

"What the hell were you trying to do?" McConnell demanded.

"Listen," Pike said, and told McConnell and Hobbs what he and Gall had talked about.

"Jesus," Hobbs said, "it makes more sense to me to get out of here now."

"Well then, go ahead," Pike said. "Make your move now. I won't stop you."

Now that Pike was telling Hobbs to go ahead and leave the man was having second thoughts.

"Staying?" Pike asked.

"I'll wait for the rest of you," Hobbs said.

"Then I don't want to hear from you, anymore," Pike said. "Just wait until you hear from us."

Hobbs fell silent, but Pike could feel that the man was pouting.

"The animals are gettin' restless already," McConnell said.

It was true. They were shifting about in the corral nervously, some of them snorting loudly.

"We can't let them out yet," Pike said. "We've got to wait. We're going to need them for cover."

"As long as we don't get stomped to death while we're waitin'," McConnell said, sidestepping an anxious horse's hoof.

Up in the bluffs the Blackfeet were holding their torches, waiting for the word from their leader to set the fires.

Their leader was a tall young brave called Dark Moon, who was holding a position high up in the bluffs, from where he could see the entire valley floor. He knew that most of the white men had dug themselves holes. He also knew that there were three of them in the corral, with the animals. Dark Moon realized that the horses and mules in the corral were a poor lot, but that was beside the point. It would still bring him prestige to take the animals away from the white man and return to camp with them.

Small Bear joined his leader, Dark Moon, and said, "All is ready."

Dark Moon looked at Small Bear. They had grown up together—as many of the young braves had—but had not particularly been friends. He knew that Small Bear was not happy that Dark Moon had been chosen to lead this particular party. The other brave was always pushing Dark Moon to make a decision *now*, while Dark Moon exhibited much more patience than Small Bear did—which was exactly *why* he was chosen as leader.

"It is time," Small Bear said.

"Not yet," Dark Moon said. "We will give them more time."

"To do what?" Small Bear argued. "Come up with a plan to escape?"

"And where do they have to go, Small Bear?" Dark Moon asked.

The other man scowled and looked away. Small Bear was anything *but* small. He was several inches taller than Dark Moon, and twenty pounds heavier. They had fought many times as children, and every time it had been Dark Moon who was left lying in the dirt. They had not fought as young men, though, and Dark Moon did not fear

Small Bear. Those childhood beatings meant nothing to him, and he was confident in his ability to overcome *any* foe in hand-to-hand combat—even Small Bear.

He thought that Small Bear knew this, *felt* his confidence, because their confrontations now always stopped short of becoming physical.

"Tell our people not to do anything until I signal," Dark Moon said, "and then I want the fires set from the far end of the valley."

"The far end?" Small Bear replied. "It will take longer for the fire to reach them."

"I know that," Dark Moon said, patiently. "Go and tell them."

Still scowling mightily, Small Bear went to do as he was told.

Dark Moon knew that setting the fires at the far end would allow the whites to watch while the fire swept in on them. Watching and waiting would cause their panic to rise, and once they panicked they would be much easier to handle. Oh, he knew that he and his braves could sweep down on them now and kill them all, claiming victory through sheer numbers, but that would not be accomplished without some casualties of their own. No, it was better to wait and pick them off without losing his own men. Returning with all of his men alive would add to his prestige, his legend, and that was important to Dark Moon. He was a very ambitious young man.

33

* * *

Pike studied the sides of the bluff, and knew that they were covered with Blackfeet. There would be a leader up there, somewhere. Where would he set up if he was the leader? Probably at some high point like . . . like there! He saw a lone brave sitting higher up on the bluffs than the rest. The more he watched the man, the more convinced he became that he was looking at the party's leader. The man never moved, was rock steady as if he was in complete control—and he was.

"What the hell are they waitin' for?" Hobbs asked aloud.

"Panic," McConnell said. "They have a patient leader, and he's waiting for us to panic." Pike knew that McConnell had also spotted the leader.

Hobbs bit his lip, wiped the sweat from his head with his sleeve, and said nothing. He was *feeling* panic, but he didn't want Pike and McConnell to know that.

Of course, Pike knew it already. He could feel the panic from the others, too, even though they were twenty or thirty feet away. He only hoped that *Gall* would be able to control them, as well as himself.

"Somethin's goin' on," McConnell said.

Pike stood up and took a look. It appeared that some of the braves were moving to the far end of the valley, carrying their torches.

34

"Where are they goin'?" Hobbs asked.

"They're going to start the fires from the far end of the valley," Pike said.

"But why?" Hobbs asked. "They could set the fires right close to us and have us smoked out in no time. Why start from the far end?"

"No," Pike said, "they have a smart leader. He wants us to be able to watch the flames moving in on us, which is just what they'll do. The breeze is blowing this way. It'll be like sheets of flames just bearing down on us. It's *sure* to cause a panic."

"The smoke will reach us well before the heat and flames do," McConnell pointed out, "carried ahead by the breeze."

"He knows that, too."

"Have you spotted him yet?" McConnell asked.

"I think so. Up there, see him?" he pointed.

"Way up on top," McConnell said, nodding, "out of our reach."

"Right."

"With a good view of the entire valley floor," McConnell said. "He knows everything that's goin' on down here."

"Yeah," Pike said, "but he doesn't know what we're thinking."

"And we don't know what he's thinkin'," Hobbs pointed out.

"Thanks, Hobbs," McConnell said.

Pike didn't say anything. He was sure he knew

some of what the brave was thinking, but Hobbs was right to some extent. There was no way they could know *everything* that he was thinking, but the same applied to him. Of course, from his vantage point the brave knew things about them that they couldn't possibly know about the Blackfeet. He could see how many of them there were, and how they were deployed. Pike could only guess how many Blackfeet there were, and where they were.

Of course, everyone knew that the Blackfeet could have simply swept down on them and killed them all, but their leader obviously didn't want to sacrifice any of his men to do that. That suited Pike just fine. This at least would give them time to try and figure out a way to outmaneuver the Blackfeet. A less patient leader would have come in and killed them all already, and to hell with the casualties. In this case, the man's patience might actually work to his disadvantage.

"Keep an eye on him, Skins," Pike said. "He'll signal those braves at the far end of the valley when to set the fires."

"Right."

Pike moved away from McConnell, sidestepping an anxious mule, until he could see Joe Gall. Gall spotted him and waved, indicating that everything was okay.

Sure, Pike thought, so far, but once they set those fires, and once the flames start sweeping in

36

on them, would they be able to hold the men back?

In his foxhole Joe Gall was trying to regulate his breathing. In and out, he chanted to himself, in and out, don't panic, don't *run,* goddamnit! It was cold out, but beneath his clothes he was covered with sweat — sweat that stank of fear!

He knew that the other men were watching him, and when he faced them he made sure there was no expression on his face. That part was easy. He was too *scared* for his face to have any movement, at all.

His hands on his rifle were wet, and he tried to wipe them off on his clothes without anyone seeing. He was sure there were others who were doing exactly the same thing. For the sake of their wives he knew that Kincaid and Walters were probably trying to seem calm.

"Jesus, Joe," the man nearest him said, "we got to get out of here."

"Not yet, Ted," he said, looking at the man. "Just stay where you are until I tell you different. Got it?"

"Sure, Joe," Ted Shaker said, "sure . . ."

Good, Gall told himself, be the boss, be in charge, stay calm . . . Jesus, are any of us gonna get out of here alive . . .

* * *

From high above the valley floor Dark Moon had watched Pike's progress back and forth, away from the corral and back. The man was very big, and he only knew of one white man that big, the one they called He-Whose-Head-Touches-the-Sky, the man called Pike. With Pike down there, there was less chance that the men would panic at the sight of the torches. Dark Moon knew now that he would have to go ahead and set the floor of the valley aflame. Once the other whites saw sheets of flames closing in on them, even the great Pike wouldn't be able to keep them from running. Dark Moon's braves would have to move quickly, though, to get the white women while they were still alive, and to get the animals before they ran off in panic.

He looked down and saw Small Bear looking up at him, waiting for the signal for the braves with the torches to start the fires.

He gave it.

Pike saw it.

"This is it," he said to McConnell. "He's given the signal."

McConnell looked up at the brave, who was now standing motionless, his arms folded across his chest. McConnell wished he could see the man's face. He had another wish, too. . . .

"I'd like to get my hands on him," he said.

"With a little luck . . ." Pike said, but then let it trail off.

It was going to take a *lot* of luck just to get out of this alive, let alone finding that particular brave afterward and getting their hands on him.

"We'll give it our best try," he finished.

"Yeah," McConnell said, "but before we can do that, we have to get out of here alive."

Pike looked at McConnell and said, "Details, details."

CHAPTER FIVE

Pike could see the flames catch in the grass. The Indian braves threw their torches away and ran back into the bluffs.

"Okay, we have to stay calm," he said to McConnell and Hobbs.

"Sure," Hobbs said, close to losing his composure already, "look at those flames."

Pike looked, and the flames, being fanned by the wind, were catching and *moving* very quickly towards them — and fanning out, towards the bluffs.

"Look," Pike said, "look, look . . ."

"The flames," McConnell said. "They're headed toward the bluffs!"

"It's going to backfire," Pike said. "Their plan is going to backfire on them. They're going to get caught in their own trap."

"Yeah," Hobbs said, "but there's plenty of flames left over for us."

What he said was true. The flames were still moving towards them at a good pace, and now the smoke was starting to roll in ahead of it.

"Let's get ready," Pike said. He looked over towards Joe Gall, hoping that the man would be able to control his own panic, and the panic of the men around him.

Joe Gall saw the flames moving towards them and climbed out of his hole.

"Joe!" someone shouted to him.

"Wait," Gall said, loud enough for all of them to hear. He was looking over towards the corral, trying to catch sight of Pike.

"Joe, we gotta run!"

"Not yet," Joe Gall said, feeling a tightness in his stomach and his chest. Jesus, he said to himself, not yet.

Dark Moon looked down at the valley floor, which was quickly being engulfed by the flames, and saw that the flames were also moving up towards the bluffs. The wind in the valley was *swirling,* and because of this the flames were not only moving forward, but fanning out towards him and his braves.

"Do you see what's happening?" Small Bear shouted up at him. "Our own people are going to be swallowed by the flames."

Dark Moon stood and faced Small Bear.

"Tell them to move now," he said.

"Move?" Small Bear said. "Where?"

"Into the camp," Dark Moon said. "Now!"

41

Small Bear shook his head, turned, and called out Dark Moon's orders to the braves in the bluffs. The braves, loyal to Dark Moon, started moving down the bluffs towards the floor of the valley.

"They're coming in," Pike said.

The smoke had reached the camp, and his eyes were starting to water. If it got any thicker, he and Gall wouldn't be able to see each other. He had to signal Gall now.

He turned, found Gall and waved his arms.

"Now!" he shouted. "Now, Joe! Now!"

Joe Gall saw Pike through the smoke and heard him shouting.

"All right," Joe Gall called out to his men, "let's move."

"Where?" someone asked.

"Just run," Gall said. "Use the smoke as cover and get away. Run now!"

The men climbed out of their holes and started running. A few, blinded by the panic that was now being released, were running *towards* the smoke and fire, and towards the Indians.

"No, the other way," Gall shouted, but they couldn't hear him.

Someone fired a shot, and then another was fired, and suddenly it seemed that everyone was shooting. . . .

* * *

Pike and McConnell kicked apart the flimsy corral and started waving their arms at the animals. They needn't have bothered. The animals were wide-eyed with fear from the heat and smoke, and needed no urging to start running. Most of them ran *away* from the fire, but some of them actually ran into the camp.

"We can't control them," McConnell said.

Pike watched helplessly as a man ran across the path of a horse and a mule, and both animals trampled him in their panic.

He felt McConnell's hand grab his arm.

"Come on, Jack," he said. "We've got to get going. There's nothing else we can do here. Hobbs is gone. Come on, damn it."

Pike started to turn towards his friend when he saw one of the women, the Crow woman Bright Deer, run into a loose horse. The animal knocked her down and kept going. She wasn't moving.

"You go on!" he told McConnell, pushing his friend. "Go!"

He didn't wait to see if McConnell started running. He ran towards the fallen woman, hoping that the animal's hooves had missed her.

When he reached her he saw that she was apparently unhurt. She had simply had the wind knocked out of her. He grabbed her arms and pulled her to her feet.

"Are you all right?"

She started to answer, but suddenly her eyes widened, and she shouted a warning. He turned and saw two Blackfeet Indians running towards them. He raised his rifle and shot one. The other brandished a knife and kept coming. Pike reversed his hold on the rifle and swung it at the brave, striking him on the side of the head. The Indians went down and didn't move.

Pike turned and saw that Bright Deer was still standing there, frozen by fear.

"Come on," he said, grabbing her hand and pulling her after him. "Come with me."

As he pulled, she followed, and he started trying to work his way through the smoke—but it wasn't only the smoke. The heat was oppressive, and it was beating some of the men back into the clearing they had used as a camp. As Pike and Bright Deer slipped away in the smoke, there were others who would never make it away at all.

After Pike left McConnell to go and help Bright Deer, McConnell had also seen people in need of help. He saw two women crouched over a fallen man and ran over to see if he could help.

"What happened?"

The women looked up at him, tears streaming from their eyes. He couldn't tell if they were crying, or if their eyes were simply streaming from the smoke.

"He won't get up," one of the women said.

McConnell bent over and saw that there was good reason why the man wouldn't get up. He had taken a shot in the back of the head, and was dead. He looked at the women, one of whom still had ahold of one of the man's arms, trying to pull him to his feet.

"Ma'am," he said, and then had to shout, "ma'am! He's dead! Let him go!"

"He can't be dead!" she shouted back.

McConnell looked at the other woman, who seemed somewhat calmer about the whole thing.

"He's her husband," she said, as the first woman fell to her knees by the man. "Her name is Alice Kincaid."

"And who are you?"

"I'm Betsy Walters."

"Where's your husband, Mrs. Walters?"

She shrugged and said, "I don't know. He ran off and left me when the Indians started the fire. He could be dead by now . . . for all I care, he could be."

"Mrs. Walters . . ." McConnell said, "you don't seem too . . ."

"Upset?" she asked. She gave him a hard look and said, "He left me behind like I was a dog, mister. I really don't care what happened to him."

When she put it that way, he could understand, and sympathize.

"But you do care about Mrs. Kincaid?"

45

"Of course I do," the woman said. "She's my friend, and she's lost her husband because he *wouldn't* leave without her. *I'm* not leaving without her."

"Then help me get her to her feet, ma'am. We've got to get out of—" He stopped short when he looked around them and saw that the clearing in which they had been camped was now completely ringed by fire.

"We have to go where?" Betsy Walters asked.

They couldn't go *anywhere*. They were completely surrounded by flames.

Because their camp was in a clearing, with hard packed dirt instead of brush, the flames could not completely overrun it. Instead, the flames moved *around* the campground, encircling the dirt clearing. Anyone who had not been swift enough to run clear was now trapped inside the clearing. This included McConnell, the two women, Joe Gall and several other men.

"Why aren't you gone?" McConnell asked Gall when the man came over to see what was going on.

"I wanted to make sure my men got away," Gall said. "It looks like not all of them did."

Betsy Walters had managed to get Alice Kincaid to her feet.

"Kincaid?" Gall said to McConnell.

"Yeah, he's dead."

"Where's Walters?"

"I don't know," McConnell said. "I don't know what he looks like, but his wife says he left her behind when the fire started."

Gall looked around them and saw that there were three other men in the camp with them.

"We can't get out now," McConnell said. "We're completely surrounded by flames."

Suddenly, they were being shot at. McConnell looked up and saw through the smoke that many of the Indians had climbed back onto the bluffs, above the flames. They were firing wildly, though, because the smoke was keeping them from getting a good bead on them. Apparently, the same ring of fire that was keeping McConnell and the others in was also keeping the Blackfeet out.

"What do we do now?" Gall asked.

We'll have to find some cover and wait out the fire," McConnell said.

McConnell looked around and saw that several animals were lying on the ground. They had either been shot or overcome by the smoke.

"Come on," McConnell said, "we'll fort up behind the carcasses."

They moved towards the dead animals, McConnell and the two women crouching behind a dead horse. Gall and one man got down behind a mule carcass, while the other two men did the same with a second one.

"Mrs. Walters—"

"Call me Betsy," Betsy Walters said, "since we're probably gonna die together."

"We're not gonna die, Betsy," he said. "Can you handle Mrs. Kincaid?"

"What is there to handle?" she asked. "We just have to let her cry herself out."

He nodded. His experience with crying women was nothing to draw on, so he decided to leave it in her hands. She didn't seem like the kind of woman who did much crying herself, but maybe she knew how to handle a woman who *did* cry.

"Mister?" Betsy said.

"McConnell," he said. "Call me Skins."

"What's gonna happen to us, Skins? Are we gonna burn to death?"

"No," he said, "the fire's not reaching us. I don't know how we overlooked the fact that dirt doesn't burn. You'd think that would be something we'd remember, wouldn't you?"

"I guess maybe you had other things on your mind," she said. She was pressed up against him, and he was conscious of the fact that she was a big, firmly built woman. Her face was black, from dirt and smoke, but he thought that she might be handsome, cleaned up some.

"What will happen to us after the fire dies down?" she asked.

He guessed that if the Indians waited around that long they'd come in and get what was left, but he didn't want to tell her that.

48

"I guess we'll just have to wait and see."

"They'll come and get us, won't they?" she asked. "I mean, look at us. There's not much we could do to stop them."

"If you're gonna look at it that way, Betsy," he said, "there ain't that much left here to interest them, is there?"

"I suppose not."

He looked at her and said again, "So I guess we'll just have to wait and see, huh, Betsy?"

"I'm sorry we got you caught here with us, Skins," Betsy said, "and yet . . . I'm not."

"I understand. It wasn't your fault, anyway," he said to her. "I couldn't very well run off and leave you here, could I?"

"Why not?" she asked. "My husband did."

He was impressed with her because there was no hint of bitterness in her voice.

"I'm not your husband, Betsy," he said.

"No," she said, "you surely ain't."

He was conscious of her hands on him, then, one on his shoulder and the other sliding around his side and resting on his chest.

Jesus, he thought, what a time for his body to react to the nearness of a woman.

CHAPTER SIX

Pike kept running, pulling Bright Deer along behind him, until he felt the heat from the fire lessen. Then and only then did he stop. When he turned to look at her he saw that she was panting heavily.

"Are you all right?"

She nodded, unable to talk because she was so winded trying to keep up with his long strides.

"Rest a moment," he said.

"I . . . am fine," she said. "You run faster than any white man I have ever seen before—almost as fast as an Indian."

He took that as a compliment.

Pike looked around, but couldn't see anyone else around. Tendrils of smoke were still hanging in the air, but they were far enough away from the fire that his eyes were starting to feel better.

"I hope the others got away," she said.

"So do I." He was more concerned about McConnell than anyone else. He had lost track of his friend in all of the confusion.

50

"I am called Bright Deer."

"I know," he said. "I'm Pike."

"Yes," she said. "He-Whose-Head-Touches-the-Sky, I know."

"Your, uh, I mean, Hobbs was all right the last time I saw him," Pike said to her, seeking to give her comfort, somehow.

"I do not care." Her face was expressionless, matching her tone.

"No," Pike said, "I guess you wouldn't. He doesn't treat you very well, does he?"

"No," she answered flatly. "He treats me like a dog. Indians do not treat white women as badly as he treated me. I hope he is dead."

"Well . . ." he said. He couldn't much blame her for that. "If he's not," he said, "you don't have to stay with him."

She shrugged her shoulders indifferently and said, "Where else would I go?"

Pike frowned and said, "Let's save that question for another time, all right?"

She shrugged again.

"Let's keep moving," he said. "Maybe we'll run into some of the others, or a horse."

"Or the Blackfeet."

"Yeah," he said, helping her to her feet, "there is that possibility, too."

Dark Moon saw what was happening down be-

51

low. Some of the whites had gotten away from the camp, and some were forted behind dead animals. He was disappointed that some of the animals had been killed. His men had fired into the smoke blindly, killing some of them. He would chastise them later.

"It is all over," Small Bear said from a point just below Dark Moon.

"Nothing is over," Dark Moon said.

"Most of the whites are getting away," Small Bear complained.

"Only if you let them," Dark Moon said.

"It is not I who let them get away," the other man said, pointedly.

"Take some braves and find them," Dark Moon instructed, giving the man a hard stare. "Leave the others here with me. When the fire finally dies down, we will go in and get the rest."

"This has all been madness," Small Bear said, shaking his head. He obviously wanted to say more, but he finally went off to do as he was told.

Dark Moon remained standing, his arms folded across his chest, looking down at the smoke-covered valley. Perhaps the plan had not worked the way he had wanted it to, but he was still convinced that he had made the right decision.

"They will not let us go," Bright Deer said to Pike as they continued on.

"I know," Pike said. "Some of them will come looking for us and for the others who got away. We'll have to keep moving."

"I am glad I am with you," she said, squeezing his hand.

He turned and looked at her.

"Why?"

"You will keep me alive."

"You think they would kill you?"

"Oh yes," she said. "The white women they will keep, but me they will kill. I am Crow. They would not want me. But as long as I am with you, you will not let them kill me."

"How do you know that?"

"You are He-Whose-Head—"

"What does that mean?"

"You are not easy to kill," she said. "Many have tried. I have heard. So, if I stay with you, and you are hard to kill, I will be hard to kill, too."

"All right," he said, waving at her to stop. "I don't know how true any of that is, but I'm going to do my best to keep us both alive."

They continued on in silence until she said, "You are worried about your friend."

"Yes," he said. "I don't know if he got away before the fire closed around the camp." He shook his head at his own stupidity and said, "We should have seen that coming. Of course the *dirt* wouldn't burn . . ."

"There was much happening," she said.

"That's no excuse," he said.

He had thought himself pretty calm during the whole thing, but maybe that had been his way of panicking. Maybe *his* panic was in not thinking entirely straight. Maybe if he'd taken more time. . . .

He stopped abruptly as she dug in her heels behind him and pulled him to a stop.

"What is it?"

"Wait," she said, her tone low.

He followed her lead and kept his voice low.

"You heard something?"

"Yes."

Either her hearing was better than his, or he was too preoccupied. He figured he'd better start paying attention to what was going on around him if he wanted to live long enough to examine his behavior later on.

They stood stock still and then he heard it too. Someone was moving, off to their left, coming in their direction—and from the sound of it, it was more than one person.

CHAPTER SEVEN

"But . . . you cannot do this," Bright Deer said to Pike.

They were hidden behind a cluster of rocks, waiting for the four Blackfeet warriors to reach them. As Pike saw it, he had two options. One was to stay hidden and let them pass by. If he did that, though, they might just meet up with them again later—perhaps at a more inconvenient moment. No, the opportunity to take care of them now was just too good to pass up—and that was option number two. He *was* going to ambush four Blackfeet warriors by himself—which was what Bright Deer was telling him he could not do.

"You cannot attack and overpower four Blackfeet braves alone," she said.

"Overpowering them will do us no good, Bright Deer," he said. "What I have to do is kill them."

"That is even more unbelievable," she said, shaking her head.

"Even for He-Whose-Head-Touches-the-Sky?" he asked, raising his eyebrows.

"You are still a white man, she said, as if that explained it all. "We should run away and try to avoid them."

He explained to her that the chance to get rid of them now was not to be passed up.

"Get rid of?" she said, tasting the alien phrase. "What if it is they who 'get rid of' you?"

"Well, that's just something I'll have to do my best to avoid, Bright Deer."

She put her hand on his arm and said, "If you will follow me, I will make sure they never find us."

"How can you do that?"

She gave him a look that said the answer should be obvious, and then said, "I am Crow, while they are Blackfeet."

"That's true," he said, touching her hand, "and I'm sure you could do that, but I'm afraid we're going to have to play this my way."

She took her hand off his arm and said, "You are like most Crow men."

"Brave? Strong?" he said.

"Stubborn!" she said, and turned her head away from him.

After they made their way through the fire, McConnell stopped pulling Betsy and turned to take a look at her. There was a small flame on the sleeve of her blouse, and he beat it out with his hands.

She watched in amazement, because she hadn't felt it there. She had felt the flames nipping at her heels, but not the one on her arm.

McConnell looked around, and then up to the bluffs. He saw the Blackfeet leader waving to his men, and he knew what that meant. Now that *they* had made their move, the Indians were making theirs.

"What do we do now?" she asked.

"I have to look for Pike."

She frowned and said, "I thought you told Gall that we were all on our own."

"This is different," he said, even though he knew he was contradicting himself. "Pike is my friend, and has been for a very long time."

"But—"

"He's probably my only real friend."

"But you said—"

"Come on," McConnell said, cutting her off. "They'll be coming after us now. We have to keep moving to stay ahead of them."

She opened her mouth again to speak, but he turned and started running, pulling her along.

Bright Deer was going to speak again but Pike quieted her by putting his hand to her mouth. When he removed it, she remained silent.

Pike knew it was important to kill the four warriors without firing a shot. Shots—even one—

57

would give their position away to anyone who was interested. He reversed the rifle in his hand, going over his moves in his mind. First the rifle, and then the knife on his belt. He had to do this *fast,* before the braves could realize what was happening.

Suddenly, the four braves were there, moving past their hiding place. Pike allowed them to pass, then stepped out and swung the rifle at the lagging brave, the last of the four. The stock struck the man on the back of the head and he went down in a heap. Pike stepped over him and switched the rifle to a two-handed grip. As the other braves turned, he struck one in the face with the rifle stock, virtually exploding his nose, and then struck the other with the barrel of the gun. The hard steel sliced open the man's forehead, and he went down to his hands and knees, blinded by the blood, stunned by the blow. Pike *and* McConnell had used their rifle in this fashion before, and it usually worked very well.

The fourth Indian was too quick, however. He backed out of Pike's striking range and started to bring up his own weapon. Pike threw his rifle at the man. As the Indian ducked, Pike pulled his knife and charged at the man. The Blackfoot brave again tried to bring his rifle to bear, but Pike ducked beneath and thrust outward with the knife. The blade bit into the man, and Pike pushed it in to the hilt, and then twisted the knife and cut sideways, gutting the man.

58

He turned quickly to survey the damage. Two of the other Indians were lying on the ground, and he felt sure they were dead. The last one, bleeding from the scalp wound, was still on his hands and knees. Before he could move, however, Bright Deer leaped on the man's back, forcing him flat onto the ground. She grabbed him by the hair, pulled his head up so that his neck was exposed and then slit his throat from ear to ear with a knife she'd picked up from somewhere.

The job done she stood up, leaned over to use the dead man's loincloth to clean the blood off the knife, and then straightened, her eyes catching Pike's and holding them boldly.

Pike checked the other men just to be sure they were dead, and then walked to Bright Deer. She was standing with her chin high, her hands on her hips, obviously proud of what she had done.

"Now what?" she asked.

He didn't know what to say to her about what she had done—or why she had done it. Was it to help him—or *them*—or was it some sort of vengeance that only she knew the reason for? She had been particularly vicious in cutting the man's throat. Perhaps it was just *because* she was Crow and the man was Blackfoot.

Well, none of that mattered now.

"We have to keep moving," Pike said. "It's all we can do."

"What about the others?"

"We're all on our own," he said, but he knew that his first concern was finding McConnell and making sure that he was all right. Once they were back together, they could worry about where to go from there.

Joe Gall ran, practically dragging a listless Alice Kincaid with him. He didn't know how he managed to get stuck with her. He also knew he could make better time if he left her behind, but he knew that he couldn't do that, not and be able to live with himself later. Besides, how would he explain to Pike and McConnell about leaving her behind? No, he was going to have to make sure that if he got away to safety, Alice Kincaid was with him.

Suddenly, Alice seemed to stumble and fall, almost dragging Gall down with her. He turned and saw her lying on the ground.

"Alice, come on, damn it—" he said, leaning over to help her up. That was when he saw the hole in her back—and he hadn't even heard the shot that killed her!

At least, he assumed that she was dead as he released her hand and started running with increased speed.

What else could he think?

Or do?

* * *

Steve Hobbs was running. He didn't know to where, he was just running. His only concern was getting away from the Blackfeet alive. *Where* to go was of little concern to him, only that he *went*.

He was looking behind him as he ran and suddenly ran into something. He bounced off and fell to the ground, losing the grip he had on his rifle. When he regained his composure enough to look, he found himself looking up at three Blackfeet warriors who had somehow gotten in front of him.

"Jesus," he said, groping on the ground for his rifle. Even as his hand closed over the barrel, though, he knew that he was too late . . . *much* too late.

Jesus, he thought, I should have been looking where I was goin'.

Dark Moon was alone on the bluffs as Small Bear approached him.

"Why have you not gone with the others?" Dark Moon asked his boyhood adversary.

"And leave you alone?" Small Bear replied. "Unprotected?"

"Am I a woman, Small Bear?" Dark Moon asked, though there was no rancor in his tone. "A squaw that needs to be protected?"

"No, of course not," Small Bear said, even though that was exactly what he meant to convey. "You are my leader, and I am concerned—"

"Go, then," Dark Moon said, cutting him off. "I want them all dead."

"Even the women?"

"Yes," Dark Moon said. At this point, he didn't care about taking the women alive. He was looking for some measure of revenge. "If they must be killed, then kill them. Just make sure that *none* of them get away."

"As you wish, Dark Moon," Small Bear said. He bowed at the waist, an insolent gesture that Dark Moon would be sure to remember.

As Small Bear made his way back down the bluffs, however, he knew that if one—just *one*—of the whites succeeded in getting away, it would reflect very badly on Dark Moon's leadership.

Very badly!

Before they continued on, Pike and Bright Deer dragged the bodies of the four braves over to their own former hiding place among the rocks. Pike wasn't exactly sure why he took the time to do that, but it made sense to hide them at the time.

After that they continued moving, not running but moving along at a controlled pace—a *quick* pace to be sure, but a controlled one. They couldn't afford to become winded and have to stop and rest. This way they might be able to keep moving, putting more and more distance between them and the rest of the Blackfeet.

Pike had decided that instead of moving aimlessly, they should head for his and McConnell's campsite, even though it was twenty miles away. True, the Blackfeet might have located their camp before they ran into them, but that was a chance he thought was worth taking. They had supplies there, and pack horses, and *their* horses might have even run back there. Me thoughts that McConnell might have the same idea.

"Where are we going?" Bright Deer asked. She had obviously realized that they were now moving towards a definite destination.

He explained where they were going, and why, and she accepted his explanations silently. It made sense to her, as well.

She was moving along easily with him, keeping pace right alongside. Pike had the sudden realization that this young Crow woman could probably run all day, running him into the ground in the process.

It was a sobering thought.

McConnell called their progress to a halt, which pleased Betsy to no end.

"Don't you ever get tired?" she asked him.

"I do," he said, "but Indians don't. We'll rest for a few minutes, though."

"Thanks," she said, trying to catch her breath. "I'd keep moving if I could—"

"It's all right," he told her.

"You know," she said, bent over with her hands on her knees, "you could go on without me. I mean, I can find my own way."

"Never mind that."

She looked up at him, still bent over, and said, "Why risk your life for me, Skins? You didn't even know me until a little while ago. You don't know *who* I am."

"Sure I do," he said. "You're a woman a man would have to be a fool to leave behind."

"And you're no fool for risking your life for me?" she asked.

"Jesus," he said, "I hope not."

She put her head down, took a few more deep breaths, and then straightened up and stared at him, her hands planted firmly on her hips.

"All right, I'm ready," she said. "Which way do we go now?"

"That way," he said, pointing.

"Why that way?" she asked. "If we go north we'll be moving even further away from the burning camp."

"Maybe so, but Pike and I have a camp up there," he said, pointing the other way again. "There's food and supplies there, and pack animals and, if I know him as well as I think I do, Pike."

"Let's go then," she said. "If there's food there, I want to get there as soon as possible. All this running is starting to make me hungry."

"My kinda woman," he said, shocking her for the moment so that she frowned at him.

"Let's go," he said.

CHAPTER EIGHT

Pike stopped abruptly, causing Bright Deer to bump into him from behind.

"What is it?" she asked.

He pointed ahead of them, and she saw that someone was lying there on the ground about twenty yards ahead of them. It was a man, and he was lying completely motionless.

"A white man," she said.

"Yes."

"It could be a trap," she said.

"I know."

"We should change direction," she said. "Go around him."

"He might be alive."

She shook her head.

"He is not."

"I have to check."

"If it is a trap—"

"I'll have to take that chance," he said. "If he's alive, he's going to need help."

"This is foolish," she said.

"It ain't the first foolish thing I've ever done," he said. "You wait here."

"No," she said, shaking her head, "you wait, and I will go first."

"Bright Deer—"

"I will look and see if it is a trap," she said.

"I can do that—"

"If there are Blackfeet around," she said, "they will not hear *me*."

He wanted to argue further, but she ran off silently, and he had no chance. He had to admit that *he* couldn't hear her moving through the brush, but then he wasn't a Blackfoot Indian. He had never argued the merits of the Crow and the Blackfeet with McConnell or anyone, but right now he hoped that the Crow were at least quieter.

He crouched down, holding his rifle in both hands, intently watching the body lying on the ground ahead of him. There was no movement at all; he couldn't even tell if the man was breathing. The odds that the man was alive were slim, but he still had to check and make sure.

As suddenly as she had left, Bright Deer was back next to him, startling him. She *was* quiet.

"There is no one else around," she said. "It is not a trap."

"Good," he said—unless the Blackfeet were better at hiding than the Crow were at finding them. He shook his head to dispel that thought and stood up. "Let's go and have a look."

* * *

Similarly, McConnell and Betsy were staring at the body of a man which they had almost stumbled over. They had no chance to wonder if it was a trap or not, for the body was just suddenly there, at their feet.

McConnell looked at Betsy and saw that she was staring intently at the man. The body was lying on its stomach, but he thought he knew who it would be even before he turned it over. He did so and saw that the man had been stabbed to death, and then scalped. His face was covered with blood that had poured down from his scalp, leaving his face a mask of red, but Betsy obviously had no trouble identifying the man.

"Is this who I think it is?" he asked her.

"Yes," she said, stiffly, looking away, "that's my husband."

McConnell released his hold on the body, and it flopped over on its back. Betsy tried to look at it, but wasn't able to and kept her eyes averted.

"Come on," he said, taking her arm and steering her away from it.

They walked several yards away and then stopped when he was sure she couldn't see the body from where they were standing.

"I'll bury him if you want," he said, "but we really shouldn't take the time—"

68

"No," she said, cutting him off. "Leave him there. We can't take the chance."

"You know," he said, "if he had taken you with him, you'd both probably be lying there now."

She took a deep breath and said, "This is probably the only time in his life he did something *for* me, and he didn't even realize he was doing it."

"How do you feel?"

She took a deep breath and let it out, hugging her arms tightly to her. She looked at him and said, "I don't know how I feel. I suppose I should feel something, huh?"

"I don't know," McConnell said, helplessly.

"Look, forget it," she said. "As far as I'm concerned, he was dead as soon as he left me back there. Let's keep moving."

McConnell put his hand on her arm for a moment, then dropped it and said, "All right, then, Betsy, we'll keep moving."

Pike and Bright Deer approached the body, and Pike turned it over.

"It's Hobbs," Pike said. "I guess I should've let him run when he first wanted to."

"This is not your fault," she said.

He stood up and said, "I know that, but I can't help but feel sorry for the poor bastard. All he wanted to do was run."

"And you should have let him?" she asked. "You saved him from being a coward."

"I'm sure he would settle for being a live coward than what he is now," Pike said.

Hobbs had been stabbed and scalped, and his open eyes stared sightlessly at the sky.

Pike looked up at the sky too and said, "It'll be dark soon. We won't make it to our camp tonight. We'll have to find someplace to spend the night."

"Take his shirt," she said.

"What?"

"His shirt," she said, and then crouched over the body to remove it, roughly. "You will need it to keep warm."

Pike didn't relish wearing a dead man's shirt, but then he figured he wouldn't have to. For one thing it would be too small for him, so he let her take it, thinking that she would be the one who ended up wearing it.

"He is wearing long underwear," she said, as she stood up.

"Never mind," Pike said. "I'm not going to strip a dead man naked."

Before leaving, though, Pike did search the area to see if Hobbs's rifle was around anywhere, but there was no sign of it, so it had obviously been taken by the Indians who had killed him.

"All right," he said, "let's go and find someplace to stay the night."

Joe Gall crouched in a fissure he had found between some rocks, his arms folded around himself to try and get some warmth. He felt badly about Alice Kincaid, and kept trying to convince himself that she was dead before she hit the ground. If she was still alive, would she *still* be alive if he went back now? No, there was no point in throwing his own life away. That shot in the back had to have killed her instantly.

He'd keep telling himself that. . . .

As darkness fell he hoped that he wouldn't freeze to death, saving the Blackfeet the trouble of finding him and killing him.

Pike wanted to stay inside a circle of rocks they had found, but Bright Deer told him that wasn't such a good idea.

"The Blackfeet would look here," she said, "and the rocks will only increase the cold. If there was heavy wind I would say yes, to protect us from it, but there won't be any wind tonight."

That made sense, he thought. How many times had he lost the skin on his hand by leaning up against a rock at the wrong time? The stone caught and held the cold for a long time.

It was Bright Deer who found a spot for them, a naturally hollowed area inside some brush which would hide them, and would not add to the cold.

The space was barely big enough for both of them, but that was okay, she said.

"We will be able to use each other for warmth," she said.

A white woman might not have been so casual

about that, he thought, even if the physical contact was only to save their lives.

Once they were hidden away Bright Deer tried to give him the extra shirt, but he told her it was too small and she did end up wearing it herself, as he'd figured. They huddled together, and he was aware of the fact that her body was very firm as well as warm. Under other circumstances being pressed up against her would have been pleasurable. Hell, even though they were only doing it to keep warm, he felt his manhood swelling—which was fine, because *it* was also warm.

Bright Deer was aware of his body's reaction to her, and she pressed even more tightly against him. Her hand fell to his thigh, and slid to his crotch where it settled over his erection.

"You are very large."

"Um, I guess."

"And hot," she said, rubbing her hand over him, "so hot."

"Bright Deer," he said, unsure of how to handle this, "this is not the place—"

"I know," she said, but she didn't remove her hand. She *did* stop rubbing him, though, for which he was grateful. The last thing he needed in this cold was to wet his crotch.

McConnell and Betsy did not find anyplace as convenient to spend the night. They finally settled for sitting on the crouch behind a few pine trees.

"We're going to freeze," Betsy said, rubbing her arms to generate some heat.

"No, we won't," he said, setting his rifle down on the ground next to him. "Come here."

She stared at him for a moment as if considering his invitation—if that's what it was—and then went and sat beside him. He put his arm around her and pulled her to him, and she sat stiffly against him.

"Relax," he said, "we need to keep each other warm or we *will* freeze."

"Yes," she said, "I understand that."

She made an effort to relax and leaned more naturally into him, and after a few moments she pressed even more tightly to him, seeking the warmth of his body. Any semblance of resistance was gone after the first half hour, and they felt considerably warmer.

For McConnell's part, he also felt his body responding again. Hopefully, she wouldn't notice and take offense. Or *would* she take offense? He recalled that moment earlier—it seemed days ago—when they were huddled together inside the ring of fire, and she had put her hands on him. Then she hadn't seemed shy about touching him.

"In the morning we'll head for the camp Pike and I made," he told her.

"And hope that the Indians didn't find it, already," she added.

"That's right," he said. "If they didn't, we should be in pretty good shape."

"And if they did?"

He shrugged and said, "Then we'll be no worse off than we are now."

They sat that way silently for almost an hour, McConnell staying alert for the sound of anyone approaching. Just when he was starting to think she might have fallen asleep, she spoke.

"I didn't love him anymore, you know."

"What?"

"My husband," she said. "There was no longer any love between us."

"Uh-huh," he said.

He didn't know *what* to say, but then he didn't think she was looking for a reply from him. She simply had some things to get off her chest.

"I hadn't loved him for a long time," she said, "but I had nowhere to go. I *had* to stay with him."

He tightened his arm around her, and she leaned her head on his shoulder.

"It's all right to cry anyway," he said, and he could feel that she *was* crying and added, "Not too much, though. The tears might freeze."

She reached up and wiped her face with her palm, an angry gesture.

"I'm *not* crying," she said.

No, he thought, not anymore.

* * *

"Pike?"

"Yes?"

"If we survive this . . ." Bright Deer said haltingly, "I think that I would like to . . . lie with you . . . be with you . . ."

"I'd like that too, Bright Deer," he said, tightening his arm around her. Her hand was still in his crotch, and he supposed that was the warmest part of either of them.

"I'd like it a lot," he added, "someplace nice and warm."

"Yes," she said, leaning her head comfortably on his shoulder. Her hand was still in his crotch. It wasn't doing anything, it was just there.

Dark Moon and his braves camped for the night, building several fires. The bluffs where they had hidden were now burning, as the flames had consumed the valley floor and then looked elsewhere for sustenance. In retrospect, Dark Moon supposed that the fire might not have been the best idea — but he'd never admit that to anyone.

"We are missing four of our braves," Small Bear said to him.

"I know that," Dark Moon said. "The whites will pay for that."

"It must have been Pike," Small Bear said. "Did you see him?"

"I saw."

75

"He-Whose-Head-Touches-the-Sky," Small Bear said, tasting the name. "To kill him would be something to be *proud* of. Women and children would sing songs about the brave who killed him."

"You will have your chance, Small Bear," Dark Moon said. "All you have to do is find him."

"I will find him," Small Bear said, "and I will kill him."

And then, he thought, we will see who the elders choose as the future leader of their people, Dark Moon or Small Bear.

CHAPTER NINE

In the morning Dark Moon woke first and then woke all of his braves. He wanted to make sure they got started before the whites did.

"We don't even know how many whites there are wandering around out there," Small Bear said as the camp came to life around them.

"How many bodies did you count?" Dark Moon asked.

"There were more than fifteen," Small Bear said, "and we found some after the fire and killed them, but we don't know how many there were to begin with."

"What about the horses?"

"We have recovered about twelve horses and seven mules," Small Bear said. "Some of the others died in the fire, and others ran off."

"All right," Dark Moon said. "All of the whites don't have to be killed, but I want Pike, and I want the two women."

Small Bear agreed—to himself, not aloud—that

this would be satisfactory—but only if *he* was the one to kill Pike.

"I want Pike alive," he said to Dark Moon, "so I can kill him."

"I don't care who kills him," Dark Moon said, "as long as he dies."

Small Bear nodded and said, "Don't worry. He will die. I will see to it."

He went to the others and let them know that anyone who killed Pike would have to answer to him.

McConnell woke and found that Betsy had somehow ended up sleeping with her head in his lap. In addition to that, his body had betrayed him while he was asleep, and he had an erection. Her knees were drawn up to her chest and her arms wrapped around them.

"Betsy," he said, without touching her. She didn't wake even after he called her name a second time. He finally had to shake her, and she jerked awake.

"Take it easy," he said, but when she realized her head was in his lap she sat up quickly, her face coloring. They were a few steps away from death, and she was blushing because she had slept in his lap—and she couldn't have *not* noticed that he was aroused. He couldn't complain, though. His lap was the warmest part of him.

"Um," she said, "did you sleep?"

"Yes."

"I'm sorry if I—" she started to say, but he cut her off.

"Never mind," he said. "As long as you slept. We have a long walk ahead of us, and we're going to have to watch out for Blackfeet."

"You don't think they might have . . . just given up and gone home?"

"I doubt it," McConnell said. "This raid didn't work out the way their leader planned. For him to go back empty-handed would be the same as going back defeated. He's got to save face by finding us."

"Us?"

"Some of us," he said, "some of the animals— and the women."

"Me and Alice."

"Yes."

"What about Bright Deer," she asked. "Hobbs's Crow woman?"

"I think it's likely the Blackfeet would just kill her."

She smiled grimly and said, "That's almost enough to make me wish I was Indian and not white. I don't relish the idea of being captured by the Blackfeet."

"Don't worry," he said. "I wouldn't let that happen to you."

"Thanks," she said. Suddenly she covered her face with her hands and said, "I must look frightful."

"You look fine," he said. He stood up and assisted her to her feet.

"I'm chilled to the bone," she said, rubbing her upper arms.

"We'd better get moving," he said. "We'll warm up some that way."

He was glad she hadn't asked him how he would prevent her from being captured by the Blackfeet. He didn't want to have to tell her that he would kill her before letting her be taken.

Bright Deer woke before Pike. She tried to get up and look around without waking him, but he stirred as soon as she moved and came instantly awake. They both crawled out from their shelter and stood up.

"Good morning," he said.

"I was going to look around."

"Don't bother," he said. "We'd do better just to get moving. We know they're going to be out there. They won't give up. Their pride won't let them."

"Oh, yes," she said, "foolish pride. That is probably the only thing that Blackfeet men and Crow men have in common."

"White men, too."

She was quick to agree.

"Yes."

Pike checked his rifle to see if the powder was dry, and decided to replace it to make sure. When

80

the gun was properly loaded he said, "Let's get moving. We'll warm up that way, too."

They walked along for a while before Bright Deer started to speak.

"I was very bold last night," she said.

"Were you?"

"I was," she said, "but we were very close to death yesterday—"

"I know."

"—and we still are, today. If we could find a place, a warm place, I would still like to do . . . what I said last night."

He looked at her, but she was looking straight ahead. He admired her body, her back straight, her breasts bold and firm, her legs long and powerful. He marvelled at how she managed to look fresh even after all they had already been through.

"So would I," Pike said. "We'll find a place, Bright Deer. I promise."

Joe Gall woke and didn't want to move. He knew if he closed his eyes he'd fall back to sleep, and then he would probably never get up again. With a groan he pushed himself up off the ground to a seated position, then stood up and stretched. Every muscle in his body protested, and he moaned aloud.

Did he dare think that maybe the Blackfeet had given up and weren't still looking for survivors?

And how *many* survivors were there, he wondered. McConnell, Betsy Walters? Was Pike alive? How many of his other men were still alive? Had he been the death of them with his foolish ideas of leaving Wynan and being a leader on his own? And what would happen when he returned to Wynan's camp? Would Nate take him back? Would the others in camp want him back with them after they heard what had happened?

Joe Gall thought that maybe it would have been better if he had died yesterday, with the bulk of his men—but he only thought that for a moment.

Aside from Pike, McConnell, and Gall, there were seven other men wandering about, trying to avoid the Blackfeet, wondering where the hell they should go.

They were travelling in three groups of two, two, and three. Two of the men were Stan Hendrick and D.J. Resnick. Another two were Roger Simon and Shad Lowell. The three men who were travelling together were the Smith brothers, Red and Jay, along with Dave Connors.

Hendrick and Resnick were hopelessly lost. It wasn't that they didn't know where they were; it was just that they didn't know where to go.

"Which way, D.J.?" Hendrick asked.

Resnick looked around and said, "I'm not sure, Stan. I think we got all turned around during the night."

"Well, we've got to pick some direction," Hendrick said. He pointed and asked, "How about that way?"

"I was thinking that way," Resnick said, pointing in the opposite direction.

The two men stared at each other helplessly. As bad a leader as they had all agreed Joe Gall was, they would have welcomed him with open arms, at that moment.

Simon and Lowell decided that they had better try to make their way back to Wynan's camp—although walking all that way seemed unthinkable. They decided that the best thing to do was look for some of the horses. They knew some were dead, and the Indians had probably caught some of them, but there might still be some wandering around free.

"It's too cold to walk," Shad Lowell said.

"And we still have our rifles," Roger Simon pointed out. "Hell, if we come upon some Indians with horses we can *take* them from them."

"Right," Lowell agreed.

After a moment Simon said, "As long as there aren't too many of them."

"Right," Lowell agreed.

The Smiths and Connors had also decided that getting back to Wynan's was the thing to do, but they were being bold about it. Since there were three of them, they still felt that they would be a match for any Blackfeet they might encounter.

"Six," Jay Smith said, "even if we come upon six of them we can take care of them."

"Sure," Dave Connors said. "Any white man is a match for two Indians."

"Three," Red Smith said.

"Right," his brother said. "Three."

So they all agreed that they were a match for anything they might run into—as long as there weren't more than *ten* Indians.

As a result of their decisions and attitudes, Resnick and Hendrick were moving tentatively, Simon and Lowell cautiously, and the Smiths and Connors rashly.

Few of them, if any, would live out the day.

CHAPTER TEN

Hendrick and Resnick were the first to die. It wasn't noon yet when they came face to face with four Blackfeet warriors, unexpectedly. Of course, it *shouldn't* have been unexpected because they were trying to be careful *not* to be found by any of the Blackfeet, but there they were, ten feet in front of them.

They hadn't made any plans for what they would do if they did encounter Indians, so they both reacted differently.

Hendrick turned and ran.

Resnick raised his rifle and shot one of the Indians in the chest. The sound echoed and was heard by everyone in the area.

So were the shots that followed, the ones that took Resnick down and killed him.

Hendrick died as soon as the remaining three braves caught up to him.

* * *

Pike stopped short when he heard the first shot. He and Bright Deer exchanged a glance after the ensuing shots.

"One shot," he said, "followed by three."

She nodded her agreement.

"Someone else has died," she said.

Pike hoped it wasn't McConnell, or Joe Gall.

"I hope he took one of the bastards with him," he said, and they continued on.

When she heard the first shot, Betsy Walters gasped and grabbed McConnell's arm.

"Easy—" he said, but the rest of what he was going to say was cut off by the next three shots, fired very closely together. Probably three rifles fired at almost the same instant.

Betsy's grip on McConnell's left arm tightened until he thought she must be cutting off the circulation of his blood.

"Take it easy," he said. "Those shots were pretty far off."

"Not so far," she said.

"All right," he said, "so I lied, but they were still somewhere else."

"I wonder . . . I wonder who's dead this time," she said.

"I don't know," McConnell said, hoping that it wasn't Pike. "Let's keep moving, Betsy."

* * *

Gall heard the shots and stood stock still until the echoes had all died out. For that moment he was frozen in place, unsure of which way to turn, which way to go. What if he went the wrong way and ran right into a band of Blackfeet warriors. Then there'd be more shots, and *he'd* be the one who was killed.

Small Bear heard the shots and hoped that Pike had not been killed. It was not likely, since all of his Blackfeet warrior brothers knew that the big white man was not to be killed.

He hurried in the direction of the shots, worried anyway. . . .

Dark Moon heard the shots and was satisfied that his braves had found at least one more white man, and maybe one of the white women. Even if they picked the whites off one by one, he would be satisfied.

Simon and Lowell heard the shots and looked at each other for a long moment.

"Shit," Lowell said.

"Yeah," Simon agreed.

After that, they moved even *more* cautiously.

87

* * *

The Smith brothers and Connors heard the shots, and Connors said, "Those sonsofbitches."

"We better know what we're gonna do if we come face to face with those bastards," Red Smith said.

"Yeah," Jay said, "let's come up with a plan of action."

The three men discussed a plan as they continued on.

A little after noon McConnell called their progress to a halt so that Betsy could rest.

"I can go on," she insisted, between gasps.

"I need some rest, too," he lied.

"Liar!"

"Save your breath," he said. "You're gonna need it. After this we won't rest until dark, or until we reach our camp."

McConnell found himself wishing they had been able to recover Betsy's husband's rifle.

"Can you shoot?" he asked, suddenly. "I didn't ask you that before."

"I can shoot," she said. "All I need is something to shoot with."

"Well," he said, "we'll have to see what we can do about that."

* * *

At the same time of the day—but miles apart—
Pike offered to stop so Bright Deer could rest.

"I am not tired," she told him, "but if you want
to stop—"

"That's all right, Bright Deer," he said. "I think I
can make it."

"Well," she said, "you *are* a white man . . ."

It was then that Pike first started to think that
maybe the Crow woman had a sense of humor. . . .

If Pike had felt the need to rest then, he would
have, even if it had hurt his pride. This was not a
time to let his ego get the better of him, but he
honestly felt fit and ready to keep moving.

If and when he didn't feel fit he would stop and
take a rest, but he knew Bright Deer would never
ask him to stop. When he started to feel the need,
he would assume that she was tired, too.

She continued on, walking ahead of him, and he
lagged behind, admiring the way she looked from
behind, admiring the way she moved. There was a
lot about this woman to admire, and he found
himself hoping that they would find that nice warm
place fairly soon.

Simon and Lowell died next.

It was late in the afternoon when they came
upon the horse. It was standing still, its head bent,
nuzzling the ground, looking for something to eat.

89

It was a particularly swaybacked beast, but they had no qualms about catching it, and riding it double until it dropped. At least that would put some distance between them and the Blackfeet — that is, if the Blackfeet were also on foot.

"Don't spook it," Simon said.

Lowell laughed.

"I think either one of us could outrun that beast, but you're right. We'll be better off if we don't have to chase it."

Together they advanced on the horse. For two men who were being cautious up to that point, they were now throwing caution to the wind. It never occurred to either of them that the horse might be a trap.

And of course, it was.

There was a volley of shots that once again stopped everyone in their tracks, and they all knew that someone — probably *more* than one — had died . . . again.

McConnell stood with his head bowed and said, "They're picking us off, one by one . . . or more."

"Should we hide?" Betsy asked. "Maybe after today they'll just stop looking."

"We need some hot food," McConnell said, "and some blankets . . . and some hot coffee! No, we can't afford to just stop and hide. We have to keep moving." He gave her a pointed look and asked, "What do you think?"

"Me?"

"Sure," he said. "Your life is at risk here, too. What do you think?"

Betsy moved close to him and slid her hand into his. Before, when he held her hand it was only to pull her along. Now, it was different, and when he tightened his hand around hers she felt reassured—slightly.

"I think we should keep moving," she said. . . .

"I wonder why they're not tracking us on horseback," Pike said to Bright Deer. He said this when he thought back to the four braves on foot that he had disposed of. Why were they on foot?

"We would hear them long before they reached us," she said. "This way there is more chance of them sneaking up on . . . on some of us."

"I guess I'm lucky I paired off with you, huh?" he asked.

"Yes," she said matter-of-factly, "you are."

Small Bear had been with the braves who had set the trap with the horse, and now looked on with satisfaction as the braves scalped the two dead whites. He knew that other braves had also killed two whites, and that of the four they had killed so far today, Pike had not been among them.

The hunt continued.

Dark Moon had remained in camp while his braves went out hunting. With him were two braves, whose job it was to look after the horses. Now he decided to mount up and ride out on the heels of his hunting braves. He would be riding far enough behind them so that their quarry would not hear him. Along the way he would be able to see just how many of the whites they had found so far and left dead.

He instructed the other braves to follow soon, bringing the horses with them.

CHAPTER ELEVEN

It was almost dark when Pike and Bright Deer reached the camp.

"Our first piece of luck," he said, regarding the camp with satisfaction.

The camp looked completely untouched. Even the mule they had fettered before leaving was still there—hungry, but still there. After all, they had not expected to be gone more than several hours.

Pike went through the camp to see if it was as untouched as it seemed. Everything was there. Their food, their coffee, their supplies, their extra powder and possibles.

And their blankets.

Bright Deer picked up one of the blankets and wrapped it around her.

"It does not look like anyone has been here," she said, looking down at the ground.

"I'll build a fire," Pike said.

"They will see it," Bright Deer said.

"I know," he said, "but we can't spend another

cold night without a fire. Besides, McConnell might see the fire, too.

"I will help," she said. She cast off the blanket and collected the makings of a fire.

Once Pike had the fire going, he made a pot of coffee, and they were both soon sipping from steaming cups. He cut a couple of strips from a chunk of venison he and McConnell had killed and skinned before they left and dropped them into a frying pan.

"I do not like coffee," she said, making a face, but she kept sipping it, welcoming the warmth.

Pike put his cup down for a moment, went to his gear and came back with his Kentucky pistol. He sat down opposite her and picked up his coffee again.

"Do you know how to use a pistol?" he asked.

"Yes."

He reached across the fire and handed her the pistol, which she accepted. She rested it in her blanketed lap and did not give it another thought.

"I'll give you what you need to reload it," he told her.

She had a sheepish look then and said, "I know how to shoot it, but I do not know how to reload."

"Don't worry," he said, "it's easier to teach reloading than it is shooting. You can either shoot or you can't, but you can be taught to load."

Pike removed the meat from the pan, handed Bright Deer a plate and took one for himself. They both ate the meat while it was steaming hot, lick-ing the grease from their fingers, and then had more coffee.

After they had eaten enough — but not *too* much, because they didn't want to get sick — he taught her how to reload the pistol. When it looked like she had the hang of it, he told her to get some sleep.

"What about you?"

"I'll keep watch."

"I will take a turn," she said.

"That's all right."

"If you do not wake me," she said, "I will wake up on my own."

"All right," he said, looking at her and knowing that she was telling the truth and that there was no arguing with her. "I'll wake you in four hours."

She nodded, wrapped herself in a blanket and lay down by the fire.

Pike sat on the other side of the fire, being care-ful not to look into it so as not to destroy his night vision. His rifle was on the ground next to him, and he put on another pot of coffee. He wanted to have a full pot there for whenever McConnell ar-rived. He was worried about his friend. As badly as he didn't want him and Bright Deer to spend another night without a fire, if McConnell was out there somewhere, he was spending a second cold night.

Pike hoped his friend was still moving, even in the dark, and that he would arrive in camp fairly soon. He and Bright Deer wouldn't be able to stay here another night, not after building a fire, cooking and making coffee. The smells would lead the Blackfeet right to them. If McConnell didn't arrive fairly soon, the camp would be useless to him, and whoever might be with him.

McConnell looked at Betsy, who was shivering.

"We have two choices," he told her. "We can stay here and build a fire, or we can keep goin' in the dark to our camp."

She was vigorously rubbing her arms with her hands, trying vainly to warm herself.

"I'll leave the decision up to you," she said, "but am I crazy, or do I smell coffee?"

He sniffed the air and said, "You have a good nose. Yeah, that's coffee. Pike must have gotten to the camp already."

"And he's built a fire and put on coffee?" she asked. "He'll lead the Blackfeet right to him, won't he? And what about us? The camp will be no good to us, won't it? Once the Blackfeet have found it?"

"Not tonight, though," McConnell said. "We must be pretty close to the camp, Betsy. Pike is cooking to show *us* the way. He wants us to get there tonight. I say we keep movin'. We can get some coffee and food and some blankets, and then abandon the camp."

"What happens if we stay here and build a fire?" she asked.

"If we don't get to the camp tonight," he said, "it may not be there tomorrow. Pike is going to have to move out. It's tonight, or not at all."

"Well, Skins," she said, "like I said before, it's up to you."

"Let's keep movin'," he said. "I don't think we'll be runnin' into any Blackfeet tonight."

"Let's go, then," she said. "The smell of that coffee is starting to drive me crazy."

Bright Deer had been asleep about an hour when Pike heard something. He picked up his rifle, stood up and moved out of the circle of the fire into the shadows. Someone was approaching the camp, and the chances were good that it *wasn't* Blackfeet Indians. For one thing, they were making too much noise—but that led Pike to believe that it might not even be McConnell, unless he had someone with him.

Pike remained in the shadows and for a moment considered waking Bright Deer, but when he looked at her he noticed that she was already awake. She was still wrapped in the blanket, but she was awake, and he knew she'd have the pistol in her hand and be ready to help.

Those approaching were very nearly there, and suddenly two figures came out of the darkness, one larger than the other. It was obvious that

they weren't Indians, but Pike raised his rifle anyway . . . and then McConnell entered the circle of
light thrown by the campfire.

"Skins!" Pike said, coming out of the shadows.

Bright Deer sat up and tossed off the blanket. In
her hand was the pistol.

Pike closed the distance between him and his
friend, and the two clasped hands. "You made it,"
Pike said.

"You knew I would," McConnell said. "I see you
have coffee ready."

Pike looked past McConnell at the woman who
was with him. He didn't recognize her.

"Pike, this is Betsy Walters. Her husband was,
er, killed."

"I'm sorry, Mrs. Walters," Pike said.

"Thank you," she said, "but call me Betsy,
please." She looked past Pike and said, "Hello,
Bright Deer."

"I will cook something," Bright Deer said, moving to the fire.

"Come by the fire, Betsy," Pike said. "I'll pour
you some coffee."

McConnell and Betsy both eagerly accepted cups
of coffee, and warmed their hands on the cups
while sipping the hot, black liquid.

"Oh, this is like heaven," Betsy said. "I've been
so *cold*."

"We've all been cold," Pike said. "Skins, who
else got away?"

"Joe Gall and some of the others," McConnell said, "but you must have heard the shots."

"Yes, we did," Pike said.

"So we don't know how many are still alive . . . or if *any* are."

"Well," Pike said, as Bright Deer tossed some slices of meat into the pan, "if they're out there, they're going to have to find their way to us."

"Unless," McConnell said, "they went in the opposite direction."

"Towards Wynan's?" Pike said.

McConnell nodded.

"If they did that," Pike said, "they're on their own."

"Jesus!"

The exclamation came from Red Smith as he turned to see what he had tripped over in the dark.

"What is it?" his brother Jay asked. Behind *him* came Dave Connors.

They had all decided that it would be to their advantage to keep moving through the night. Of course, they were more *stumbling* than moving, and now Red Smith had stumbled over something, and when he looked down he saw a body.

"A dead man," Red Smith said.

"Shit," Jay Smith said. He leaned over and tried to see the man's face. "It looks like Simon."

"Lowell's over here," Dave Connors said from a few feet away.

"Scalped?" Jay Smith asked.

"Yep," Connors said.

"Here, too," Red Smith said.

"Those sonsofbitches!" Jay Smith said.

The brothers exchanged a glance and said, "Do you think they're still around?"

"They must have camped somewhere by now," Connors said, but his tone was more hopeful than positive.

"Shit," Red Smith said, "what do we do now? Keep moving or camp somewhere?"

"It's too cold to camp," Jay Smith said, "unless we build a fire."

"We might as well keep moving and try to stay warm that way."

"Warm?" Red Smith said.

"Well, warmer than we'd be if we made a cold camp," Connors said.

"Shit," Jay Smith said.

Dave Connors thought that must be a favorite word of the Smith brothers.

Joe Gall was in a similar position. He did not want to make a cold camp, and he did not want to take the chance of building a fire. That left continuing to travel in the dark as the only option open.

Jesus, he thought, if I *ever* get back to Wynan's, I'll never again think of being booshway of my own camp . . ."

* * *

None of these men were anywhere near Pike and McConnell's camp, they could *not* smell the coffee or the cooking meat, and they were actually moving in the opposite direction.

Small Bear sniffed at the air, smelling a white man's camp, and Dark Moon noticed.

"I smell it, too," Dark Moon said.

"That way," Small Bear said, pointing. "If we break camp and move tonight—"

"There is no need," Dark Moon said. "They cannot escape now."

"If they have food to cook, they might have other supplies, as well," Small Bear said.

"But not horses," Dark Moon said. "They will still be on foot tomorrow, and we will be on horseback."

Dark Moon had his braves camp for the night, but Small Bear was chafing, wanting to continue to hunt even in the dark.

"We know where they are now," Dark Moon said, looking in the direction of Pike and McConnell's camp. "They cannot escape."

"And the others?" Small Bear asked. "There are still others who may not be camped, but still moving through the night."

"We will send some braves in the other direction,

101

just in case," Dark Moon said, "but the rest of us will track Pike, and the women. They cannot escape us," he added, again.

Small Bear hoped that was true, but he was loyal enough to his chosen—or *appointed*—leader that he gave up the argument.

Dark Moon was still the leader . . . for now.

CHAPTER TWELVE

With McConnell in camp there was no need for Bright Deer to take a turn on watch. It took Pike a little time, but he finally convinced her of that. When both women were bedded down, McConnell sat with Pike for a while, exchanging stories and discussing their situation.

"So how many of the others do you figure got away?" Pike asked.

"Well, when we were ringed by the fire there must have been at least ten of us," McConnell figured. "What about you?"

"It's hard to say," Pike said, thoughtfully. "We don't know how many were killed, and there was a lot of smoke. When Bright Deer and I got away, I wasn't looking around to see who else had."

"What a mess it turned into," McConnell said. "That fire really got out of hand."

"Yeah," Pike said, "but if the Blackfeet *hadn't* set the fire we might *all* be dead, right now."

"Instead of *nearly* all," McConnell said.

"I think we'd better just assume that only the four of us are left, and concentrate on getting ourselves out of here," Pike said.

"So where do we go?" McConnell asked. "Nate Wynan's camp?"

"He's probably closer than any settlement," Pike said, "but in order to do that we'd have to go back the way we came."

McConnell raised his eyebrows and said, "The Blackfeet sure wouldn't be expectin' that. From here they'd just expect us to keep on goin'."

"That's right," Pike said, thoughtfully. "They would, wouldn't they?"

"I never did get a good look at their leader," McConnell said. "It sure would help us to know who he was. If we *knew* him, we might be able to predict what he was going to do."

"I think we have to figure that he's going to keep looking for us," Pike said. "He'd lose face if he went back to his village totally empty-handed."

"Then we'll have to break camp early," McConnell said, "because they're sure to know where we are by now, if only by the smell."

"We'll leave before first light," Pike said. "We'll have to carry as much as we can, the four of us, and leave the rest behind."

"It sure would help if we had some horses," McConnell said. "What do we do about the pack mule?"

"He'll slow us down," Pike said.

"He could carry more than we could."

"And the more he carried, the slower we'd be able to go," Pike said. "No, I think we'll just have to carry only what we really need and leave the rest — and the mule — behind."

"One of us could ride the mule and maybe go for help," McConnell said.

"You want to go?"

"No," McConnell said, "I figure we got a better chance of survivin' if we stay together. I was just makin' suggestions to hear myself talk."

"Maybe we should give Betsy and Bright Deer the option of taking the mule," Pike said. "One of them might be able to get away."

McConnell turned and looked at where the two women were lying, then turned back when he was satisfied that they were asleep.

"We can ask them in the mornin'," he said. He was sure Betsy would want to stay with him — just as Pike was sure that Bright Deer wouldn't leave on her own. She probably felt that *Pike* had a better chance of surviving with her than without her.

"You'd better turn in," Pike said. "I'll wake you in a few hours."

"All right," McConnell said, getting to his feet. "Make sure you leave me some coffee."

"I'll make a fresh pot before I wake you," Pike promised.

The two men stared at each other for a few moments. They were very happy to see each other, each glad that the other had survived; they simply didn't know how to put it into words.

"Well . . . good night," McConnell said.

"Good night, Skins."

After three hours Pike made sure he made a fresh pot of coffee and then woke McConnell for his watch.

"Hear anything?" McConnell asked as they changed places.

"Not a thing," Pike said. "It's all quiet."

"I thought the Blackfeet might try to play with our minds a little."

"Well," Pike said from inside his blankets, "if they had a prisoner I guess they'd be using him for that, so we'll take this as a sign that they *don't* have any prisoners."

He had settled into the same blankets McConnell had been using, because they were already warm.

McConnell looked over at the two women, who were still asleep. They must have been exhausted—at least, he knew Betsy was. Bright Deer, being Crow, could probably walk farther than all of them, but she appeared to be just as fast asleep as the white woman.

McConnell put his rifle down next to him and poured himself a cup of coffee. He drank it scalding hot, not even blowing on it.

An hour later he was dropping fresh grains into

another pot of water when he thought he heard something. He cocked his head and listened intently, and heard it again. He picked up his rifle and stood up, his head still cocked—and there it was again.

A horse—at least *one* horse—and it sounded like a shod horse, which meant it wasn't an Indian pony. Of course, that didn't mean that there couldn't be an Indian riding it.

McConnell moved over to Pike and nudged him with his foot. Pike came awake, almost instantly.

"What is it?" he asked.

"Listen."

Pike listened for a moment, then got to his feet.

"A horse?"

McConnell nodded.

"Sounds like it's shod."

"We'd better be careful, anyway," McConnell said. "Let's move away from the fire."

"I'll get the women."

Pike knelt over Betsy and Bright Deer and woke them both. Bright Deer came awake, instinctively holding her tongue. Pike had to put his hand over Betsy's mouth to keep her from crying out.

"Someone's coming," he told them. "Move away from the fire."

"To where?" Betsy asked.

"Come with me," Bright Deer said, taking Betsy by the arm. Pike nodded to her, and then went to stand with McConnell.

107

"How do you want to do this?" McConnell asked.

"One of us out of camp, and one in," Pike said. "I'll move out and see if I can't take whoever it is by surprise. If I take him, I'll call out."

"I'll be ready."

They nodded to each other, and then Pike melted away into the darkness.

Pike moved through the brush as quietly as he could, stopping every few yards to listen. He also stopped and waited until his vision adjusted to the total darkness. He could still hear the horse and was now sure that there *was* only one horse.

He listened further, located the source direction and started moving that way. When he was sure he was only yards from the horse, he stopped and waited, as the animal was moving towards him.

He waited . . . waited . . . waited and then there was the horse, moving towards him at a slow walk, and there was no one on it. It was not only not being ridden, but it was unsaddled and—as it came closer—he realized that it was McConnell's horse.

He stayed where he was and did not move towards the animal. The horse had sensed his presence and had stopped and was waiting, but Pike wanted to be sure that this wasn't a trap. The Blackfeet could have sent the horse ahead of them to try and draw somebody out.

While the horse stood stationary, Pike began to move around it, searching the brush for a trap. He made a complete circle around the horse and did not approach it until he was sure that only he and the horse were in the area.

"Easy, boy," he said, but he needn't have bothered. The horse was standing stock still, its sides heaving, and was showing no sign of shying away from Pike. It was thoroughly soaked and had probably walked a long way over the past couple of days, making its way to their camp by a roundabout route.

Pike grabbed a handful of the horse's mane and then slowly walked it back to the camp.

"Skins, I'm coming in!" he called out before entering the camp.

"That's my horse," McConnell said as Pike and the animal came into the light. "What kind of shape is he in, Pike?"

"Let's check him out," Pike said.

They did and it seemed to be in fine shape, aside from the fact that it was tired.

"I'll rub him down," McConnell said.

"I'll have some coffee," Pike said. Bright Deer and Betsy came over, and Pike said, "You ladies might as well go back to sleep."

"I feel like some coffee," Betsy said.

Bright Deer made a face but said, "I will also have some. She didn't like the taste, but she enjoyed the warmth it brought her.

The three of them sat down at the fire and drank coffee while McConnell cared for his horse.

When McConnell returned to the fire, Pike handed him a cup of the hot liquid as he sat down.

"Well," McConnell said, "now we have a horse."

"One horse doesn't help much," Pike said, "unless we intend to split up."

"Why would we split up?" Betsy asked.

"Well," Pike said, looking at McConnell, who nodded to him, "you and Bright Deer could take the mule and the horse and move a lot faster without us."

"No," Betsy said, just a split second before Bright Deer said the same word.

"We should all stay together," Betsy said.

"All right," Pike said, "let's figure out how to play this, then."

"If we're goin' to use the animals," McConnell said, "—and I think we have to, now—I think Betsy and Bright Deer should ride the horse, and we'll load some supplies on the mule."

"We have to be ready to cut the mule loose, though, if we have to run," Pike said. "That means the women should have some supplies on the horse with them, and we should be carrying some. We'll use the mule for supplies we don't *have* to have, so that we won't mind if we have to lose them by cutting him loose."

"Okay," McConnell said, looking at the women, "what do you think of that?"

"I can walk," Bright Deer said.

"We know that," Pike said, "but why walk when you can ride?"

"We should take turns riding," Betsy said. "Why should Bright Deer and I be the only ones to ride? We're all dead tired."

"Maybe we're all tired, but you're women and we're men," McConnell said.

"What's that mean?" Betsy asked.

"Let us be gentlemen, Betsy," McConnell said. "It doesn't usually happen, and it may never, ever happen again."

Betsy looked at Bright Deer, who didn't seem inclined to get involved in the discussion. She just looked back at Betsy and shrugged.

"Oh, all right," Betsy said, "as long as we stay together."

"Bright Deer?" Pike said.

She nodded wordlessly. She didn't seem to have a lot to say about anything.

"All right, then," Pike said to them, "you ladies can get another hour's rest before we start moving. You'd better take it."

Pike thought Bright Deer might want to argue further—-or at least discuss it further or say *something*—but she simply shrugged, and she and Betsy returned to their blankets.

"I wonder . . ." McConnell said.

"You wonder what?"

McConnell looked at Pike and said, "I wonder where your horse is."

111

"We'll just have to make do with the one that we have, I guess."

"That was a joke, Pike."

Pike looked at McConnell and said, "Oh, that's just great."

"What is?"

"Now I'm losing my sense of humor."

CHAPTER THIRTEEN

The morning brought more surprises . . . for everyone. . . .

Dave Connors woke up and stared at the sky for a moment. It was almost light. Wasn't he supposed to be awakened to stand watch?

"What the—" he said, sitting up.

He looked around and saw that both Smiths were wrapped in their blankets. One of them was supposed to wake him when it was his turn to stand watch.

"Hey!" he shouted, but neither of them stirred. He threw his blanket back and got to his feet. He took a moment to stretch, and rub his eyes, and then walked over to where the brothers were lying.

"Come on! What's goin' on? We have to get movin'," he said. He nudged Red Smith with his foot and said, "Wasn't you supposed to wake me up?"

Red didn't move.

"Red? Jay?"

A coldness forming in the pit of his stomach, Dave Connors leaned over, put his hand on Red Smith's shoulder and turned the man over. Red's mouth was closed, but beneath his chin was a big, red, gaping hole. It was like a second mouth, mocking him.

"Jesus!" Connors said, backing away from the dead man. In doing so, he tripped over Jay Smith and fell onto his butt. "Jay, wake up! Somebody cut Red's throat."

Still seated, he reached for Jay's shoulder and turned him over. There was an identical red yaw underneath *his* chin.

"Ahh!" Dave Connors screamed. He backpedalled fiercely, rubbing his butt on the ground as he tried to get away from the second dead man. How had someone managed to sneak into camp and cut both their throats without waking him? *Who* could do something like that?

The answer was simple.

Indians.

Connors jumped to his feet and started running. He left his rifle behind. He didn't know where he was running to, he was just running as hard and as fast as he could to get away from his dead colleagues, and the Indians who had killed them. . . .

Small Bear was amused.

During the night he had decided to take some

braves and have a look around. They found the place where the three white men had decided to camp. They had obviously grown too tired to go on, and had left one man on watch. That man, however, had been drifting off to sleep, and it was a simple thing to sneak up on him and slit his throat. That was when Small Bear got the idea to slit the second man's throat, and leave them for the third man to find.

Now, as the third man ran screaming from the camp, Small Bear turned to the three braves with him and smiled at them.

"Catch him, kill him, scalp them all and then see if there are any others around," he said. "I am returning to camp. The rest of us will continue to search for Pike and the others."

The three braves, all on horseback, took off after the man. Small Bear mounted his own pony, turned it and rode back to camp to tell Dark Moon that three more whites had been removed.

Pike and McConnell were loading the pack mule when they both heard a horse approaching.

"I don't believe it," McConnell said as Pike's horse walked into camp.

"Why not?" Pike asked. He was surprised himself, but tried not to show it. "Do you think your horse is smarter than my horse?"

"Not smarter," McConnell said, grinning, "but I guess faster."

Bright Deer went to Pike's horse and walked it over to him.

"Smarter," Pike said. "He took his time getting here and isn't so used up—are you, boy?"

He checked the animal out and found it to be unhurt, except for a few scratches on one foreleg.

"We don't have time to let your horse rest, Jack," McConnell said. "We've got to get movin' now, before the Blackfeet get here."

"We'll walk him with us for a while, before we ride him," Pike said. "At midday we can stop for a rest. After that we can start using him."

"Agreed, but let's get movin', now," McConnell said. "They could be along anytime."

"It's too bad we don't have our saddles, also," Pike said.

"We could probably get them," McConnell said.

"How?"

"Go back to Gall's camp," McConnell said. "They probably weren't damaged by the fire, because they were inside the camp, where the flames couldn't get at them. At the very worst they smell like smoke, but they're still there."

"Unless the Blackfeet took them."

"The saddlebags, and everything in them, maybe," McConnell said, "but what would a bunch of Blackfeet Indians want with a couple of saddles?"

"Good point," Pike said.

"If we're plannin' on doubling back that way anyway . . ." McConnell said, shrugging.

"Why not?" Pike asked.

* * *

Joe Gall had kept moving through the entire night, and by the time the first light started to dawn, he was practically sleepwalking—but at least he was still alive.

That was something. . . .

It didn't take long for Dark Moon, Small Bear, and their braves to find Pike and McConnell's camp.

Small Bear dismounted and put his hand over the dead fire.

"It is still warm," he said. "This is where they were last night."

Dark Moon looked around from astride his pony while Small Bear studied the ground.

"They have horses!" he exclaimed, scowling.

"Where could they have gotten horses from?" Dark Moon asked.

Small Bear made a circuit of the camp and found the tracks of the horses coming into camp, and then going back out.

"Their own horses," he said, then. "The animals must have instinctively made their way back here."

"They would be used up," Dark Moon said. "They wouldn't be riding them. Not yet. We can still catch up to them. Which way have they gone?"

Small Bear came over and stood in front of Dark Moon's pony.

"They are going back the way they came," he said, "and we came."

Dark Moon frowned.

"That does not make sense."

"Of course it does not," Small Bear said, triumphantly. He was pleased. *He* understood what was happening, and Dark Moon did not. In front of all the braves, he would have to explain it to *their* leader.

"That is why they are doing it."

"But why?"

"That large white camp?" Small Bear said . "The one you decided was too large and well-manned to attack? That is where they are going."

"Then we must catch them before they get there," Dark Moon said. "If they reach it —"

"— we will either have to let them go, or finally attack that camp," Small Bear finished. He leaped astride his pony, looked at Dark Moon and added, "But, of course, that will be *your* decision."

"This was a good idea," McConnell said.

"And it was mine," Pike said.

"No, it wasn't," McConnell said. "It was mine."

"Come on now," Pike said, "admit it. I thought of it first."

"I *said* it first."

"Are you fellas always like this?" Betsy Walters asked, shaking her head. "There are about forty Blackfeet down there looking for us. If they heard, or looked up here and saw us —"

They had gone to higher ground to keep an eye on

their camp. It was Pike's idea—and McConnell knew that—to watch the camp so they would know just when the Blackfeet found it. Watching would further tell them which way the Blackfeet would go in their search for them. They had made tracks as if they were doubling back, hoping this would confuse the Indians. Maybe they wouldn't *believe* that the whites really would double back, or maybe they would split their force and go both ways—back the way they had come, and the opposite direction—and that would give them fewer Indians to worry about.

"You know," McConnell said, "if you had thought of this before we left camp, we could have left tracks going both ways."

"If *I* had thought of it sooner?" Pike asked. "What about you?"

Betsy looked at Bright Deer and rolled her eyes. The Crow woman simply shrugged, as if to say, "Men."

Red or white, they were all the same.

"They could have left those tracks to deceive us," Dark Moon said.

"How did they get out of camp going the other way, then?" Small Bear asked.

"Perhaps further along they turned back—" Dark Moon started.

"We'll only find that out by following the tracks to that point," Small Bear said.

Dark Moon thought it over and said, "If they did

turn back, then we will be wasting time following their false trail."

"Give me ten braves, then," Small Bear said. "I will follow the trail while you continue on. If, as you say, they turn back, then we will catch up to you. If we do not, and you find no trail, then we will know that I am on the right trail."

Dark Moon thought it over for a short while and then nodded.

"Very well," he said. "Take ten warriors and follow the trail."

Small Bear chose his braves, calling them by name, and they started riding after the trail. Dark Moon waited until they were out of sight and then led his braves in the other direction.

They watched as the Blackfeet discussed the situation—that is, the leader seemed to be discussing it with another brave. The second brave seemed to be doing most of the talking. He was also the one who had been reading the sign they had left.

"Can you see any faces?" Pike asked.

"No," McConnell said. "I can't tell who either of those braves are."

"Would you know who they were if you could see them?" Betsy asked.

"We might," McConnell said.

"And if you did?"

"It might help," Pike said. "If we knew who we were dealing with, and what kind of man he was, it would help us a lot."

After some discussion the second brave took ten Indians and started following their trail. Pike and McConnell had left several false trails further on which they hoped would confuse the Blackfeet — even if only for a short time. The other brave — the leader — took the rest of the Indians and went the other way.

"Well, good," McConnell said. "Somethin's worked in our favor. They've split up."

"When he finds our false trails, it'll only slow them down a little," Pike said. "I have a feeling that brave — " he said, pointing down at the Blackfoot who had been doing all the talking to the leader, " — knows how to read sign real well."

"Well then, let's get down from here and get moving," McConnell said. "Our false trails will keep him circling to the west for a while, while we circle to the east. By the time he gets to *this* point, we'll have put some distance between us."

"Hopefully," Betsy said.

"By the time they get back on our real trail," McConnell said, looking at her pointedly, "we'll be on horseback."

"Making good time," Pike said. He didn't mention that they wouldn't be making *great* time, not with the horses carrying double, but they should make better time than if they were on foot.

"Let's go," Pike said. "We may just get out of this mess."

CHAPTER FOURTEEN

Joe Gall had been going in circles.

Well, that's what he got for walking through the night. Without sleep, he had just about *fallen* asleep on his feet, and when he saw a familiar landmark, the realization that he had been walking in a circle almost woke him up completely.

Almost.

It took the body to *really* wake him up.

It was lying there just ahead of him, and there was a pool of blood around it, soaking into the ground. For a moment he almost started running the other way, but that was ridiculous. This was obviously one of his men, and he had to see who it was.

He approached the body and saw that there were flies on it. For some reason that angered him. When he reached it, he swatted them all away, leaned over and turned the body onto its back.

It was — or had been — Dave Connors. He'd been scalped, hastily, and that was the reason for all the blood. When an Indian did a really neat job of scalping, it wasn't always this messy.

"I'm sorry, Dave," Gall said, kneeling next to the body.

It occurred to him at that moment that this could be a trap. He knelt there, staring down at the dead man, wondering if there was an Indian — or Indians — taking a bead on his back right at that moment. He waited, expecting to be shot in the back, and when it didn't happen he decided to chance a look around. He turned his head, looked around him, then struggled to his feet because his legs were feeling weak.

He looked around him again and decided that he had just nearly scared himself to death. There was no trap, there was only Dave Connors, and he was dead.

And Joe Gall was alive — and awake.

Finding Dave Connors and very nearly frightening himself to death was like cold water in Joe Gall's face. He was awake now, and alert, and he knew in what direction he had to go to get to Nathan Wynan's camp, and that was what he was going to do. And when he did find the camp, he was going to force Nate Wynan to come back here with his men to try and find and save whatever survivors were left — and maybe they'd wipe out some Blackfeet sonsofbitches while they were at it.

It only took an hour for Small Bear to realize what had been done.

"Pike is clever," he said aloud, staring down at the ground. This would have been Pike's idea, of that he was sure.

"What did you say?" the brave nearest him asked.

123

His name was Wild Dog.

Small Bear looked at Wild Dog, who was his age, and said, "This man I seek, Pike, he is a white devil. He would have us going in circles, if he could."

"I have heard this about He-Whose-Head-Touches-the-Sky," Wild Dog said. "Is he as great as they say he is? As hard to kill? What has he done?"

"Look, Wild Dog," Small Bear said, pointing to the ground, "look for yourself."

Wild Dog looked at the ground, but there was nothing there that would tell him why Pike was a white devil. He could not read the ground as well as Small Bear could, and they both knew it.

"I do not understand," he admitted.

This was one reason why Small Bear liked Wild Dog, and always included him when he was allowed to take a group of braves under his charge. Wild Dog was as honest as anyone Small Bear had ever met — a quality Small Bear wished he possessed. He wished he could be totally honest, for instance, when speaking to Dark Moon.

"No, you would not understand," Small Bear said. "You would have to be watching the ground for the past hour to know what I know."

"And what is that?"

"Pike has set several false trails for us, to keep us busy."

"Then he has gone ahead and not back?" Wild Dog asked. "Dark Moon is on his trail?"

"Dark Moon," Small Bear said, "is following a false trail — or, even better yet, *no* trail. Pike and the others *have* doubled back, and are probably heading back to the burned-out valley."

"But why?"

"Because he thinks that he can fool us into believing that he would *never* do that."

Wild Dog shook his head and said, "I am a simple man, Small Bear. This is too confusing for me. Tell me what we are going to do."

"We are going to stop following these trails," Small Bear said, "and go straight back to where all of this all started."

"And when we get there?"

Small Bear smiled and said, "Then we will wait."

At noon Pike suggested they stop and rest. He got no argument from anyone.

"No fire, though," Pike said, "as much as I know we'd all like some coffee."

Bright Deer made a face. She would not miss the coffee. If it was made she would drink it because it was hot, but she didn't mind the fact that they weren't going to make any.

Pike and McConnell checked on their horses and decided that the animals were ready to be ridden.

"Double?" McConnell asked. "Or should we let the women ride them while we walk."

Pike frowned, looking behind them. He wished he knew how long their false trails would keep the Blackfeet busy. If they had hours, then he'd just as soon walk while Betsy and Bright Deer rode, but he didn't think they had hours. If they had an hour they were lucky.

"I think we'll have to risk riding double, Skins," Pike said. "We need to make up some ground fast."

McConnell patted his horse's neck and said, "I'd hate to ride these animals into the ground, but I don't think we have much choice. I agree we should all ride."

"Done," Pike said.

They rested for a short while, and then McConnell mounted his horse, and Pike leaped astride his. McConnell reached down and pulled Betsy up behind him, while Bright Deer sprang nimbly onto Pike's animal. Both women put their arms around their men, Bright Deer with the mule's lead rein in her right hand. She had Pike's Kentucky pistol tucked into her belt, and in this manner they continued to ride toward Joe Gall's now burnt-out camp.

Dark Moon was not happy. He knew, as did all of his braves, that by now Small Bear must be on Pike's real trail. He did not like having to turn back, because it was admitting that he was wrong, but he had no choice. He did, however, turn his men wordlessly and lead them back the way they had come, and *they* all knew better than to say anything.

For Small Bear's sake, Dark Moon hoped that his boyhood rival would be as smart when they were rejoined.

Joe Gall couldn't believe his eyes. Ahead of him, grazing at whatever it could find, was a horse.

Now this, he thought, *could* very well be a trap. He had to stop himself from running up to the animal and leaping upon its back. He had to make sure that he could do so without being immediately shot from the animal.

He started to circle the horse—much as Pike had done the night before—and did not approach it until he was sure there were no Indians hiding nearby.

When he reached the animal, he put his hand out, and it nuzzled, as if looking for a treat.

"Sorry, old fella," Gall said, for this was one of his party's older animals, "I don't have anything for you. I don't know how strong you are, fella, but you're gonna have to carry me for as long and as far as you can. What do you think?"

The animal cocked its head and studied him.

"Yeah," Gall said, "that's what I think, too."

He rubbed the animal's nose, then climbed atop it. The horse was slightly swaybacked; it was probably one they had used as a pack animal. It probably hadn't had a man on its back in some time, but it reacted fairly well to Gall's presence. Maybe it knew that if it got Gall to where he wanted to go, it *would* get some kind of a treat.

Gall wrapped one hand in the horse's mane and then kicked it lightly in the ribs with his boot heels.

Let's see, he thought, how far we get before one of us collapses.

Small Bear called a halt to the progress of his braves and motioned Wild Dog over to him. He waited while the brave rode to his side.

"Yes, Small Bear?"

"I want you to ride back and find Dark Moon and the others," Small Bear instructed him. "Tell him that we are on Pike's trail—the real trail. Tell him to try and catch up to us."

"Tell him?" Wild Dog repeated. He did not think it his place to *tell* his leader anything.

"Tell him that I said to try and catch up to us, Small Bear said, rephrasing his comment. "After all, it is I who have found the real trail."

Wild Dog nodded, and waited to see if Small Bear had anything else to say.

"We will continue to follow the trail until you return with Dark Moon. Well . . . go!" Small Bear said, and Wild Dog rode off.

Small Bear, of course, had no intention of waiting for Dark Moon to arrive with his braves. He wanted to catch up to the whites before Dark Moon caught up to him. Once he and *his* braves caught up to Pike, he would simply kill the big white man, and any others who were with him. He did, however, want to rub Dark Moon's nose in the fact that it was *he* who was right about which trail to follow. He also wanted all of the other braves to know it, too.

Small Bear turned to regard the other braves in his charge and said, "We continue."

CHAPTER FIFTEEN

If they'd had an extra horse, Pike would have taken it and ridden to check their back trail. As it was he kept turning and looking behind him.

"You and Pike expect them to catch us, don't you?" Betsy asked from the back of McConnell's horse. "You expect them to catch us and kill us?"

McConnell, too, had turned several times to look behind them.

"We don't *expect* it," McConnell said, "but we want to be ready if they *do* catch up to us. After all, the odds *are* in their favor."

"Ready for what?" she asked. "To die?"

"Where did you learn to be so negative?" McConnell asked.

"From my husband."

"Well, he's dead, Betsy," he said. "That's where his outlook on life got *him*. It's time for you to take a new outlook on life."

"That's kind of hard considering the situation we're in right now."

"What's that got to do with it?" McConnell said.

"Your outlook should improve the harder your situation gets, not the other way around. I don't know about you, but I want to live through this."

"Skins," Betsy said, "we could be dead in a matter of hours from now."

"So?" he said. "How does that differ from any other day?"

"What?"

"On any given day you could die, Betsy," McConnell said. "Especially in these mountains. A bear, a fall, an Indian, what's the difference? That's no reason to expect it."

He felt her arms tighten around his waist as she considered his words.

"Maybe it's that way for a man," she finally said, weakly.

"And why should it be different for a woman?" he asked her.

"I don't know," she said, and he could feel her shrug, "maybe it just is."

He decided to give her some more time to think about it, and they proceeded to ride in silence.

Pike and Bright Deer were riding ahead of McConnell and Betsy Walters, and could not hear their conversation. When Pike turned to look behind them, McConnell frowned and shook his head. Pike decided to leave checking their back to McConnell, since he was riding drag.

It was getting on towards evening, and they had to decide what they were going to do, keep riding or camp. Pike reined his horse in and waited for McConnell to ride up next to him.

"It's gettin' to be that time, huh?" McConnell asked his friend.

"What time?" Betsy asked.

"Time to decide whether we camp or not," Pike said. He looked at McConnell and asked, "What do you think?"

"I think we camp and give the horses time to rest, McConnell said.

"I agree," Pike said. "I also think I'd like to double back on foot a ways and check our back."

"I can do that," McConnell said.

"My idea," Pike said, and McConnell relented.

"Let's find a place to make camp," McConnell said. "We'll get a fire started and tend to the horses while you take your walk."

"Don't get *too* comfortable," Pike said. "If I see company coming, we're gonna have to move again, and fast. Keep the horses saddled. They can rest just as well that way."

"Whatever you say," McConnell said.

They rode on ahead until they came to a clearing, in which they decided to camp. Pike handed his horse over to McConnell, hefted his rifle and started walking back the way they had come.

"Pike."

He heard Bright Deer's voice and turned.

"I should come with you," she said.

"I know I'm only a white man, Bright Deer," he said to her, "but I think I'd better do this alone."

"Be careful," Betsy called to him.

"I will."

He walked for a good half hour until he spotted

some high ground that would give him a good look at their back trail. He climbed until he had a clear look at the way they had come. There was just enough light for him to see, and he was satisfied to see . . . nothing. If the Blackfeet were coming after them — and he was sure they were — they still had a way to come.

Before he worked his way back down, darkness fell.

It was dark when Pike returned to camp, and he sang out loud and clear to keep from being shot. As he approached the fire, Bright Deer handed him a cup of coffee. He had been able to smell it from far off and had been looking forward to it.

"So, what's the verdict?" McConnell asked.

"It looked clear as far as I could see," Pike said, "which was pretty far. Unless they travel through the night, I don't think they'll get here before morning."

"Well, that's good," Betsy said, "isn't it?"

"It is if Pike's right," McConnell said. "We'd better leave before first light, anyway, just to be on the safe side."

"Still, we seem to be pretty safe for tonight, don't we?" Betsy asked.

"Pretty safe," McConnell said.

"Agreed," Pike said, "but we'll still stand some watches."

After a dinner of coffee and some dried beef, they discussed how to spend the night.

"I'll take the first watch," McConnell said, "and wake you in four hours."

"Why don't we take two hour watches?" Betsy suggested. "All four of us?"

Bright Deer nodded her agreement, and both Pike and McConnell wondered if the two women had discussed this already.

"Uh, that sounds like a good idea," Pike started to say, "but, uh—"

"You don't think I'll do a good enough job," Betsy said.

"Betsy—" McConnell said, but she cut him off.

"No, no, I understand," she said. "You and Pike are experienced and Bright Deer is—well, she's Bright Deer, but you yourself—" she said, looking at Pike, "—said the Blackfeet weren't around. I mean, I could take the first watch. What could happen during the first two hours? They couldn't possibly catch up to us in the first two hours, right?"

Pike and McConnell exchanged a glance.

"You two could use the extra sleep," Betsy said, "and I want to do my part."

Pike and McConnell still weren't convinced.

"Bright Deer," Betsy said, "help me out here."

"She is right," Bright Deer said. "You do need the rest. I can stand watch with Betsy, and we can each take three hour watches."

McConnell looked at Pike and raised his eyebrows. That sounded like a solution to him.

"That's all right with me," Betsy said. "Bright Deer can show me what to do, and then tomorrow I can take a turn alone. What do you say?"

"It sounds all right to me," Pike said, looking at McConnell.

"Me, too," McConnell said, reluctantly.

"Good!" Betsy said, clapping her hands. "At last I'll be able to feel useful."

"We will take the first watch," Bright Deer said, "and wake you in three hours."

Pike and McConnell agreed. Before turning in, they checked the animals to make sure no injury had been sustained during the day, and to make sure they were securely picketed. Because Bright Deer already had Pike's Kentucky pistol, McConnell gave Betsy his rifle, which she once again said she knew how to shoot. Thanks to McConnell, she also knew how to reload, as well.

All that done, Pike and McConnell settled into their blankets and tried to sleep. They each swore to themselves that they would sleep with one eye open, but before long they were asleep—with both eyes shut!

Small Bear knew that if he and his braves travelled through the night, they would make better time, but he also knew that it was difficult—even for an Indian, *and* even for a Blackfoot Indian—to read sign in the dark. In the morning, at first light, they would pick up the trail once again. Besides, he really wanted to catch up with Pike—the great "He-Whose-Head-Touches-the-Sky"—in the daylight. He wanted the white man to see what was coming, *and* he wanted to see the look on the man's face when he realized he was going to die.

CHAPTER SIXTEEN

Betsy woke Pike for his turn on watch.

"Did you hear anything?" he asked, rolling out of his blankets.

"No, I didn't hear anything," Betsy said, and Bright Deer nodded her agreement. "Everything seems to be very quiet out there."

"Just animals," the Crow woman said.

"All right," he said. "The both of you better get some sleep. We can't count on having an easy night tomorrow night. They're bound to close in on us by then."

"How long before we reach Nathan Wynan's camp?" Betsy asked.

"I don't know, Betsy," Pike said. "I'm not sure exactly where Nate is camped. We'll just have to keep going until we find him."

The look on Betsy's face said that didn't sound very promising.

Betsy gave McConnell's rifle to Pike, but when Bright Deer offered him back his Kentucky pistol, he shook his head and told her to keep it.

"Sleep with it," he told her, and she nodded.

While the two women settled in, Pike poured himself a cup of coffee.

Betsy was worried. She didn't hold out much hope of getting to Nate Wynan's alive, and she didn't want to die. She was unfulfilled as a woman, and didn't want to die that way. She hadn't been happy with her husband. They'd had no children, and sex between them was not good. Usually her husband would just roll on top of her, grunt and groan until he was satisfied, and then fall asleep.

She turned over and looked at Skins McConnell, wrapped in his blanket. She had the feeling that McConnell would know how to treat a woman, how to make her enjoy sex as much as he enjoyed it. Would she die before she ever found out what that was like?

She lay awake for an hour, then looked over at Bright Deer, who seemed to be asleep. Pike was sitting at the fire, looking out at the darkness, occasionally sipping from a cup of coffee.

McConnell's breathing was even and deep, and she hated to wake him, but this was something she needed to do before she died.

As quietly as she could she rolled from her blankets and moved over to where McConnell was lying.

Betsy didn't know it, but Pike was acutely aware of everything that went on round him. He chose, however, to let her do what she had to do. After all, there *was* a possibility that they would be dead by tomorrow.

Besides, he laughed to himself at how his friend must feel, being awakened the way he was. . . .

Bright Deer also knew what Betsy was doing. The two women had talked while they were on watch, and what the white woman had talked about was being unfulfilled.

"I don't know how it was with you and your man, Bright Deer," Betsy had said, "but mine approached sex the way he approached hunting — for his own satisfaction."

"All men are like that," Bright Deer said.

"Do you think so?" Betsy had asked. "Do you think Pike would be like that? I don't think Skins would. Don't we deserve to enjoy sex just once before we die?"

Bright Deer did not reply. Sex had never been something the Crow woman enjoyed, but she had already made it known to Pike that she would like to have sex with him. In a way, both women were thinking the same things, and now it was Betsy who was the first to actually *do* something about it.

Bright Deer turned over so that she could watch Pike's back, and so Betsy could do what she wanted to do unobserved.

"Skins," Betsy said.

Skins McConnell woke with Betsy Walter's breath warm on his ear. He responded the very first time she called his name.

"Betsy," he said. "What's wrong? Is it my turn on watch — "

"No, no," she said, speaking gently, soothingly into his ear. "Pike is on watch, and still has a couple of hours to go."

"Oh," McConnell said, "then what—"

"I want to share your blankets," she said.

"What? Betsy—"

"I'm cold," she said, "and I'm frightened."

McConnell stared at her for a moment, then looked over at Pike and at Bright Deer. Both were looking as far away from him and Betsy as possible, which led him to believe that they were deliberately averting their eyes. Was he the last to figure out what Betsy had in mind?

"All right," he said. He opened his blankets and said, "Come on in."

Betsy slid in beside McConnell, and he folded the blankets around them. She was a solid-bodied woman, with firm breasts and wide hips. She was *very* warm, and she smelled good, even after days on the run. He wondered briefly how *he* must smell, but then decided that men and women must smell differently to each other. Another woman might not like the way Betsy smelled at that moment, but he did.

She pressed her face into his neck, and her breath was hot on him. Her hand was on his chest, and a couple of her fingers slid inside his shirt.

"Betsy—"

"We might be dead tomorrow, Skins," she said in a whisper. "I don't want to die without ever . . . without us ever . . ."

"Betsy," he said, "your husband has only been dead a short—"

"He's been dead a long time to me, Skins," she said,

and then she talked to him a little about what her life had been like with Ted Walters — what *sex* had been like with her husband.

"I don't want to die never knowing," she said. She pushed her hand so that a button on his shirt opened and her whole hand slid inside. She kissed his neck, her mouth hot and avid. He lowered his head so that he could kiss her mouth, and her tongue blossomed sweetly against his. His hand was on her back, and he slid it down to the firm mounds of her buttocks.

"Oh God," she said, "how do we get out of these clothes?"

"Slowly," he said, kissing her mouth again, "very slowly."

And slowly they did it, helping each other, peeling their clothes off but keeping them under the blankets with them, so that if Pike or Bright Deer looked over at them they'd present an odd picture, two people wrapped in lumpy blankets.

But finally their clothes were off, and their flesh was pressed together. Her breasts were round and firm, and her nipples hard as he slid his palms over them.

His penis was rigid, and she closed both hands around it, moaning as she touched it.

"How can we —" she started, but he rolled onto his back, taking her with him. Neither of them bothered looking over at Pike or Bright Deer anymore.

She was lying atop him now, and he lifted her hips and then brought her down on him. She was so wet that he slid right into her, and she gasped, kissing him so that her cries would be muffled by his mouth.

He began moving his hips, and Betsy thought she would die. Already she knew that this would be the best sex she ever had. Her husband had *never* gone this slow. He would just pound into her as hard and as fast as he could, as if he couldn't wait to get it over with, and then he would roll off of her and fall right to sleep. She would lie awake, sometimes for hours, crying silently . . . but no more. . . .

McConnell pressed his hands to her buttocks, and her breasts were flattened against his chest. After a few moments they found the right tempo and moved their hips in unison. McConnell was so deep inside of her that she imagined she could feel him between her breasts. When she wasn't kissing him, she was biting his neck and shoulders to keep from crying out, and finally she just groaned aloud as they exploded together. She rode the waves of pleasure mindlessly, and then suddenly became awake again to the fact that they were not alone in camp. She sneaked a look over at Pike and Bright Deer, but thankfully neither of them was looking their way.

"Do you think they heard?" she asked, her mouth pressed to his ear.

"Of course they heard," McConnell said, laughing softly. "They're not deaf, you know."

She lay her head against his chest.

"Embarrassed now?" he asked.

"Oh no," she said, rubbing her hands up and down his thighs. "I'm happy now."

He cupped her buttocks, kneading them.

"Happy?"

"Well," she amended, "as happy as someone can be in our situation. Skins, I never knew sex could be like that. I never knew that I had *never* really had sex before, not really."

She kissed him then, and he tasted her tears on her mouth.

"I *really* don't want to die now," she said. "I mean, I never *wanted* to die, but I was almost resigned to it. Now I'll do whatever I have to do to go on living."

McConnell was glad to hear her talking like that.

"We'll all do that, Betsy," he said, "and we'll make it. You'll see."

She sighed and closed her eyes sleepily, and in moments she *was* asleep. . . .

CHAPTER SEVENTEEN

Pike was grateful when McConnell and Betsy fell asleep. Listening to their lovemaking had both embarrassed him and aroused him. He would have liked nothing better at that moment than to go and join Bright Deer in *her* blankets, and he was sure Bright Deer felt the same way. Maybe, he thought, when his watch was over. . . .

When his watch *was* over, he wondered how he would wake McConnell without embarrassing Betsy Walters, who was still lying with McConnell. He needn't have worried, though, for as he approached them, McConnell's eyes opened, and he nodded to Pike that he knew it was his turn.

Pike went back to the fire. Behind him he heard McConnell say something to Betsy, and then his friend joined him at the fire.

"You dog," Pike said to him.

"Hey," McConnell said, "the lady climbed into my blankets with me and practically raped me."

"Sure."

"Didn't you hear my cries for help?"

"I heard you," Pike said, "and I heard her, and it didn't sound to me like either one of you was calling out for help."

"Hey," McConnell said, "what can I tell you? Go and join Bright Deer in *her* blankets."

"That would be admitting that *I* expect to die before this new day is out," Pike said, "and I don't. I fully expect—no, *intend*—to go on living."

"Well, you won't if there's no coffee left in this pot," McConnell said.

"I made a fresh pot," Pike said. "Enjoy it. I'll see you in a few hours."

Pike's intention had been to go right to sleep, but no sooner had he rolled himself up in his blanket than Bright Deer was at his side.

"I do not think we can wait for that warm place," she said to him.

"Bright Deer," Pike said to her, "there's time for this."

"I know," she said, "but I do not wish to wait any longer."

Pike looked over at McConnell, who was looking in the other direction, and then shrugged. If it was good enough for McConnell and Betsy, why wasn't it good enough for him and Bright Deer.

"All right," he said, opening his blanket.

Bright Deer surprised him by discarding her clothing *before* she joined him in the blankets. McConnell would have gotten an eyeful, if he had been looking that way.

They were near enough to the fire that the flames gave her skin a burnished glow. She had small, firm, rounded breasts, a small waist and graceful hips. Her legs were long and powerful. Pike caught his breath at the sight of her, and then she was lying beside him, her flesh burning hot even as it was showing gooseflesh from exposure to the cold.

He folded the blanket back around them and kissed her. Her hands hurriedly undid his shirt and removed it, only she chose to drop it outside the blanket. She did the same with his trousers and boots, and the rest of his clothing until they were both naked. Pike was so big that there was barely enough room for both of them under the blanket. Occasionally, over the next few minutes, the blanket would slip aside, exposing them to the weather and to either McConnell or Betsy's eyes, had either of them been looking.

McConnell was studiously trying to *avoid* looking, while Betsy pretended to be asleep and *was* watching, with amusement. She wished she had been as bold as Bright Deer in disrobing before she joined McConnell in his blankets. She admired Bright Deer's naked form, wishing she had such a slender waist.

Pike was admiring Bright Deer's slender form, too, but with his hands. He slid his hands down her back to the gentle swell of her buttocks. He slid one finger along the crease, then reached further down until he found her moist portal. He stroked her and her breath quickened. She kissed him, thrusting her tongue into his mouth and wiggling her hips.

Pike removed his finger, grasped her hips, lifted her and brought her down on him. Her breath escaped from her in a long hiss, and he groaned himself as he felt her heat and wetness envelop him. They began to move together, her hard nipples scraping against his chest, her mouth eager on his, their groins rubbing and pressing together tightly.

Bright Deer began to speak in a low whisper, but she was speaking in her language, the language of the Crow. Pike could only catch a word here or there, but enough to know that she was urging him on. He felt himself beginning to swell, and then she was writhing on him as her time came. He exploded inside of her then, and they almost lost their blankets completely as they blindly reached for their peaks.

Pike gathered the blankets around them hastily afterward, but not before the cold air chilled their sweaty bodies. He then put his arms around her, holding her close. They stayed that way without speaking until her breathing became deep and even. He didn't think he'd be able to fall asleep with her lying atop him that way, but before long he was aware of movement. He opened his eyes and saw McConnell standing above him. First light was about half an hour away, and it was time to get moving.

Dark Moon was unhappy.

He knew that Small Bear had sent Wild Dog to taunt him with the news that they had picked up Pike's trail—or a trail Small Bear *thought* was Pike's.

There was no guarantee that Pike was even still in the area, and either way Dark Moon might come out ahead. If they did catch Pike, and Small Bear killed him, it would be a triumph for Dark Moon's leadership. If they did *not* catch Pike, Dark Moon could blame it on Small Bear.

First light was fast approaching, and Dark Moon told Wild Dog to rouse the other braves. He wanted to catch up to Small Bear before Small Bear caught up to his prey.

Small Bear had his braves up and ready to travel before first light. He assumed that the whites would be doing the same, especially if Pike *was* among them. He-Whose-Head-Touches-the-Sky would not be caught unawares. He was too experienced for that.

Small Bear knew that Dark Moon would also be on the move early. By now his "leader" must be panicking, thinking that Small Bear was closing in on Pike without him.

And with any luck, he would—today!

As Pike, McConnell, Betsy, and Bright Deer broke camp, there was very little conversation going on among them. Bright Deer and Betsy seemed to be avoiding each other, possibly out of embarrassment over what had happened during the night.

Pike himself was a little uncomfortable about having given in to Bright Deer—and to his own desires—

after what he had said to McConnell about it. Also, he had the feeling he and Bright Deer had made much more noise than McConnell and Betsy. He knew that later, when they were all out of danger, he'd hear about that from his friend.

When McConnell finally spoke, it was to make a suggestion.

"Maybe one of us should ride back again and take another look."

Pike agreed, but not immediately.

"I don't think they will have closed a lot of ground overnight," he said. "Why don't we wait until mid-day?"

"All right," McConnell said, "but this time I'll do it."

"That's fine with me," Pike said, "but let's get moving. First light is not far off."

CHAPTER EIGHTEEN

They stopped at noon to rest the horses — and Betsy. Pike, McConnell, and Bright Deer all knew that they were travelling at Betsy's pace. Of the four of them, she was the one who tired most easily. She knew it, and tried not to show it, but they stopped to give her a rest, anyway.

"I'm really fine," she said, but she said it between gasps of breath.

"That's all right," McConnell said. "I've got to check our back trail again, anyway."

"We'll wait for you here," Pike said.

"Half an hour," McConnell said. "Just give me half an hour. If I'm not back by then, start movin'. I'll catch up to you."

"Right."

"That's silly," Betsy said, shaking her head and giving Pike a look like he had just grown a second head. "We'll wait for you."

McConnell looked at her, then took her arm and walked her away from Pike and Bright Deer.

"Betsy, if I don't get back in half an hour it will be for one of two reasons. Either I can't get back, or I don't want to."

"Why would you not want to?"

"I may not have the information we need yet," he said. "There could be any number of reasons why I won't *willingly* be back in that time."

"And *unwillingly?*"

"If I'm in trouble," McConnell said.

"If you're in trouble," she said, "we'd have to help you."

"If I'm in trouble, you won't know anything about it," he said.

"We will if you're not back," she said. "We'll come looking for you."

"No, you won't," McConnell said, even though he knew that what she was saying made perfect sense to *her*. "Pike won't do that. He's got to get you and Bright Deer to safety. Besides, I wouldn't want Pike to risk his own life."

"That's bull," she said. "You and Pike have been friends a long time. I can see how close you two are. You've probably risked your lives hundreds of times for each other, and you'll do it again."

"All right," he said. "I'll let Pike argue with you half an hour from now . . . if I'm not back."

"Save us all the trouble," Pike said, coming up behind them, "and *get* back here by that time."

McConnell looked at his friend and said, "I'll do my best."

"Oh," Pike said, "well, in that case you might not be back for days."

* * *

Forty minutes later, McConnell was hoping that Pike and the women had moved on, like they planned.

McConnell had ridden back on their trail, and somehow he and a group of Blackfeet had managed to totally miss each other. It was when he was *returning* — and on time — that he saw them, and they were *between* him and his friends.

McConnell couldn't explain how it had happened, but it had. He was cut off from the others, and to get to them, he'd have to fight his way through ten Blackfeet braves. So he decided to tag along behind the Indians for a while, and that was when he realized that the Indians — if they kept moving in the direction they were presently moving in — would without a doubt catch up to Pike and the women, probably before nightfall.

Pike and Betsy had the argument she had feared they would have, and she lost.

"We're moving on," Pike said. "Skins will catch up to us."

"And if he doesn't?" she asked.

"We'll have to deal with that when the time comes, Betsy."

"And who says when it comes?"

"I do."

She turned away from him and said, "I'm goin' back for him."

He grabbed her by the arm.

"On foot?" he asked. "Without a weapon? What good would you do him?"

"More good than *you're* doin' him," she said, accusingly. "You're supposed to be his friend."

Pike looked at Bright Deer, as if silently imploring her to take over. Bright Deer walked over to Betsy, put her arm around her shoulder and walked her away from Pike. The two women conversed in low tones for a few minutes, and then returned to Pike.

"Are we ready to move?" Pike asked.

Betsy looked away from him, but Bright Deer nodded and said, "We are ready."

McConnell followed along behind the Indians for an hour. He didn't keep them in sight, but kept on their trail. If he tried to keep them in sight, they would either spot him, or hear him. The fact that they *hadn't* heard him up to this point was probably because they were so intent on looking in front of them that they weren't looking—or listening—for someone coming up behind them.

After two hours, McConnell was starting to worry. The Blackfeet were moving at a much better pace than Pike and the women were. It became clear to him that he was going to have to do something to distract them, and at the same time alert Pike to the fact that they were there.

Of course, the fact that McConnell wasn't back yet told Pike something, already.

* * *

"Well?" Betsy asked. She folded her arms and looked at Pike expectantly.

Pike turned and looked behind him, making a face. If McConnell would show up right then, it would save him a lot of grief, but he knew that wasn't going to happen.

"He's in trouble," he finally said.

"At last," Betsy said, throwing her arms up. "Are we goin' back for him?"

"No," Pike said, shaking his head.

"Wha—"

"I am," he went on. "You and Bright Deer are not. You two are to keep moving forward."

"But what can you do alone?" she asked.

Pike gave her a long, hard look and said, "A lot more than I could do with you along, Betsy, believe me."

"But Bright Deer could be a help to you, right?" Betsy asked.

"She could—"

"Then take her with you."

"She has to stay with you," he said. He looked at Bright Deer and said, "Don't you?"

She didn't answer, but he could see that she didn't necessarily agree with him.

McConnell had taken his rifle, and Pike had to take his, so all he had to leave the women was the Kentucky pistol that Bright Deer already had.

"Keep moving forward and don't turn around no

matter what happens. He was speaking more to Bright Deer than to Betsy.

"Are you going on foot?" Betsy asked.

"Yes."

"But . . . take the horse. We can walk."

"I'm better off on foot," he said. "If I use the horse, and there are Indians close on our trail, they'll hear me coming for sure."

That made sense, even to Betsy.

"Remember," he said, before leaving them, "keep going no matter what you hear."

McConnell hated to shoot a man in the back, even an Indian that he knew would kill him if he had the chance, so he fired his shot in the air.

The Indians turned at the sound of the shot, and he made sure that they saw him before he turned his horse and started off at a gallop.

He could tell that they were coming after him.

When Small Bear heard the shot, he turned immediately and looked behind them. He saw the white man, and before he could give the order, his braves started off after the man. Of course, his order would have been for them *not* to chase the white man. The only reason the man could have had for shooting at them at that distance, and missing, was because he *wanted* them to follow him.

Small Bear saw the white man clearly enough to know that it was not Pike. He also knew that they were following a trail that was becoming more and more fresh. If he had been able to, he would have kept some of his braves from chasing the man, but their reaction was instant, and one of reflex. In the end, he too rode after them. The trail would still be there later.

Pike heard the shot and stopped in his tracks. There was just the one shot, with no volley following it. It could have been a lot of things, including a warning shot to him and the women.

He hoped that if Bright Deer and Betsy heard the shot, they would do as he told them and keep going. He himself continued in the direction he had been going, but now he was running.

When they heard the shot, Bright Deer reined the horse in, and both women turned to look behind them.

"We should go back," Betsy said. She was seated behind Bright Deer on the horse, which meant that the Crow woman had control over the animal.

"No," Bright Deer said. "We keep going, like Pike told us."

"They could both be in trouble, Bright Deer," Betsy said, plaintively.

"They will do better if they do not have to worry

about us," the Crow woman said. "Also, it might have been a warning shot."

"To warn who?"

"From Skins to Pike," Bright Deer said, "or from Pike to us. There were no shots following it."

"I still think we should go back," Betsy said, stubbornly.

"We would do more harm than good," Bright Deer said. "We will keep going."

McConnell had been planning his escape route during the last hour that he followed the Blackfeet. He had instinctively known all along that he would have to divert their attention in order to give Pike and the others time to . . . to do what? To get away? They weren't going to get away, not with the Blackfeet this close on their heels. They needed the time to dig in someplace, either to hide, or to prepare to try and hold the Blackfeet off—and that was a laugh, wasn't it? How could they expect to hold off ten Blackfeet braves? And there were probably more on the way, as well.

If he kept to a straight line in his flight, he figured to find out just how *many* more were coming. No, his plan was to flee in a circle, hopefully working his way back around the Blackfeet and getting back with Pike and the women. Of course, the success of that plan depended on how smart the Indians chasing him were.

Pike stopped running. McConnell was on horseback, and the Blackfeet were undoubtedly on horseback. He could run all day, but he wasn't going to catch up with him unless they were riding in his direction—and if that happened, it would be *them* who had caught up with *him*. No, what he had to do now was get to higher ground and hope he could see what was going on.

"There!" Bright Deer said, pointing.

"What?" Betsy asked.

"Do you see those rocks?" Bright Deer asked. "They are perfect, almost like a natural wall."

"What about it?"

"We can wait there for Pike and McConnell."

"Wait?" Betsy asked. "I thought you said—"

"I said we would do more harm than good to go back," the Crow woman said. "We have found a good place to make a stand, now. When they come back, if the Blackfeet are close behind them, they will need that."

"I see, Betsy said. "So this is a logical decision on your part."

"Of course."

"And you're not worried about them at all?"

"No."

Betsy dropped down to the ground, slapped Bright Deer on the thigh and said, "Sure."

* * *

Pike found himself high enough ground to be able to see for miles—and what he saw he didn't like.

He couldn't see faces, but he knew that the lone figure he saw riding a horse was McConnell. A couple of hundred yards behind McConnell were about eight or nine Indians—most likely Blackfeet braves. Lagging behind those eight or nine was a tenth brave. Was he the leader, or just a straggler?

Pike watched for a few moments, helpless to do anything else. After those few moments, he thought he knew what McConnell was up to. He seemed to be riding in an arc, and it was Pike's assumption that McConnell was trying to get himself turned around, to come back this way again.

Pike scrambled down from his vantage point. He had to get back to the women, and they had to find themselves a place to dig in. Pike did not see any other braves save for those nine or ten, so they would not be as hopelessly outnumbered as they could have been.

If—*when*—McConnell worked his way back to them, Pike intended to be dug in well enough to stand off ten Indians.

CHAPTER NINETEEN

McConnell thought his luck was holding. He was finally headed back the way he had come, and the Blackfeet were still behind him. They hadn't figured out what he was doing. If and when they did, he was sure they'd try to cut him off, but that didn't seem to be happening.

He hoped that the shot he had fired had alerted Pike and the women to the danger and that they were long gone. Of course, he knew that if it was Pike who was in trouble, he would never run out on him, not even if he'd been told to. He knew that Pike was probably coming up with some kind of plan that would end up getting them all killed — but would he himself be doing anything different?

He *could* have led the Indians completely in another direction, away from Pike and Betsy and Bright Deer, but he was trying to get himself back on line to eventually run into Wynan's camp. To do anything else would be suicide, and he just wasn't the suicidal type. He knew he'd *risk* his life for

Pike, but he didn't think he'd ever just throw it away for him.

So he continued to ride, knowing that eventually he'd catch up to Pike, and by that time Pike would have figured out some kind of a plan.

He hoped.

When Pike caught up to Betsy and Bright Deer, he was pleasantly surprised. The women had found perfect cover for what he had in mind, and he told them so.

"It was Bright Deer's idea," Betsy said. "Even though she wasn't worried about you."

"Whatever the reason was," he said, "it's a good spot, and a good decision."

There was even a place, off to one side, where they could leave the horses and the mule, and the animals would be partially hidden. Pike secured the animals over there and then rejoined the women behind the rocks.

"If only we could have picked up some extra guns along the way," he said.

"I'll throw rocks at them," Betsy said, only half kidding.

"That may be what we end up getting down to," Pike said.

"Pike," Betsy said, her tone worried, "what if Skins misses us? I mean, he rides right by us without seeing us here?" Betsy asked.

159

"He won't," Pike said. "He'll ride back here in a straight line."

"But he *could* miss us."

"If I have to jump out and grab him, he won't," Pike said, and that seemed to satisfy Betsy.

"How long do you think it will be before he gets here?" she asked.

"That depends on how far and wide he has to go to get turned back around," Pike said. "I'd say he should be here within the hour." He looked at Bright Deer and added, "We'll have to be ready to give him some cover."

"I will be ready."

He turned to Betsy and said, "You better find yourself some good sized stones."

Too late Small Bear realized what the white man was doing. He was leading them in a circle, until he was riding back the way he had come. Even if he had figured it out earlier, there was no way he could have gotten his braves turned around. They were hot on the white man's tail, and they smelled blood. He, however, pulled his pony up, turned it, and started to ride on what he hoped was an intercept course with the white man.

McConnell saw a familiar landmark, which meant he was finally back on course. That was good, because his horse was tiring. He could feel the animal weakening underneath him. He only hoped that the horse would last a little longer, just until he caught up to the others.

Small Bear's shortcut did not allow him to cut the man off, but he did manage to get right behind his braves. Of course, he realized later, if he'd been able to get *between* the white man and his braves it would have saved them some trouble.

Pike heard a horse and held his hand up to signal for silence.

"One horse," Bright Deer said, and he nodded.

"Coming fast," he said.

"There!" Betsy said. "It's Skins."

They all stood up and began waving their arms, and McConnell saw them. He rode his horse over to them and dismounted.

"They're right behind me," he said.

"I know," Pike said. "I counted nine or ten."

"I didn't have time to count," McConnell said.

He scrambled behind the rocks while Bright Deer took his horse over to where the others were picketed, and then rejoined them.

"You picked a good spot," McConnell said to Pike.

161

"Bright Deer found it after I went back looking for you."

"You went looking for me?" McConnell asked, frowning at his friend.

"That's what I said," Pike replied. His tone said he didn't want to discuss it.

Before McConnell could speak again, they heard the sound of horses approaching.

"Get ready," Pike said. "We're going to have to make them stop, or they could overrun us."

McConnell put the rifle to his shoulder and said, "We'll stop 'em."

Betsy, empty-handed and helpless, decided to do the only thing she *could* do—pray!

As the Blackfeet rode into the clearing, Small Bear saw where the whites were and knew that he and his braves had been lured into a trap. He reacted instantly, turning his horse and saving his own life. The ball that would have struck him instead hit his horse in the neck. On either side of him, however, a brave went down, and he shouted to his men to retreat.

As the braves came into view, Bright Deer, unaccustomed to the pistol, rushed her shot, and her ball struck a horse instead of its rider. The horse remained upright but would probably die soon.

Pike and McConnell took their time, squeezed off their shot and each struck a Blackfoot brave from his pony. After that, the other braves turned and fled—but not for long.

"They'll be back," Pike said, "as soon as they re-group."

"I am sorry," Bright Deer said, looking down at the weapon in her hand. "I missed."

"You hit a pony," Pike said, "only because the brave turned it at the last moment. I have a feeling that was the leader."

"I should have waited," she said. "Had I killed him we would be in a better position."

"Never mind," McConnell said. "Let's just get re-loaded and be ready for them when they come again."

The two braves they had shot were not moving, so it was a safe assumption they were dead.

"We've got eight to deal with now," Pike said. "If they keep charging us, we'll be able to pick them off."

"They won't, though," McConnell said. "They'll either try and circle around us, or they'll just wait until the rest of their men get here."

"We can't wait that long," Pike said. "If the others do get here, we'll be hopelessly outnum-bered."

"We're not now?" Betsy asked.

"Eight to three," McConnell said, "is not bad. Pike and I have been in worse situations before and come out of them."

Betsy didn't say what she was thinking, which was that maybe their luck was due to run out.

Small Bear barely got off his pony before the animal fell to the ground, dead. Around him his braves were dismounting and looking to him for guidance. He ignored them for the moment. Before he could guide them, he had to get his own bearings.

They were still eight, facing what sounded to him like three weapons. Among the eight of them, he and two others had rifles. The others were armed with only bows and arrows. The whites had good cover from which to fire, but he knew that if he and his braves charged them, they would lose three men. It would then be a matter of hand-to-hand, five against three at best — or four to three if he stayed back. On the other hand, if they waited for Dark Moon and the others, they would then have a much more superior force to attack with.

The smart thing seemed to be to wait, but before he made that decision, Small Bear wanted to find out who they were dealing with. If it was Pike, then he would not hesitate to sacrifice every man he had with him to kill the big white man.

"Why do you think they split up?" Betsy asked.

"We left enough false trails to explain that," Pike said.

"And once the others realize they're following false trails?" she asked.

"They'll come back this way," he said.

"And we have to get out of here before they get here," McConnell said.

"How do we do that?" Betsy asked.

"That's something we'll have to decide later," Pike said.

"And we don't have much time to come up with a plan," McConnell said.

"Oh, I don't know," Pike said. "I don't think these seven or eight will be in a hurry to charge us. Not yet, anyway."

"So what do we do?" McConnell asked.

"We come up with a plan," Pike said.

"I hope it's a good one," Betsy said.

Pike and McConnell exchanged a glance, and then Pike said, "That's usually the only kind we use."

CHAPTER TWENTY

Small Bear gave his braves their instructions, and then waited while they moved into position. On one hand he would like to have waited a long time before attacking. That would give the whites time to think about their deaths. On the other hand he wanted to have done with them *before* Dark Moon could catch up to them.

While the braves moved into position, Small Bear decided to try and find out whether he was dealing with Pike, or not.

Small Bear spoke the white man's language, although his command was limited.

"Can you hear?" he called out, loudly.

When someone shouted out in English, "Can you hear?", Pike and McConnell exchanged a glance.

"Should we answer?" Betsy asked.

"Shhh," McConnell said.

"We hear you," Pike called back.

There was a moment of hesitation.

"Are you Pike?" the voice called.

Pike didn't answer right away.

"Are you He-Whose-Head-Touches-the-Sky?" the voice then asked.

"Who is *that?*" Betsy asked McConnell.

He knew she wasn't asking who the Indian was.

"It's a name the Indians have given Pike," he explained to her, "because he's so tall."

The voice called out again, asking the same question.

"I don't know if it will work in our favor or not," McConnell said, "but maybe you should go ahead and answer him."

"I am Pike," Pike finally answered, then reluctantly added, "He-Whose-Head-Touches-the-Sky."

His statement was greeted with silence.

"Do you want me?" Pike shouted.

Silence.

"If you want me," Pike continued, "then let the others go."

"Whoa!" McConnell said.

"No," Bright Deer said.

Betsy didn't comment.

"If they're interested in me—" Pike started, but McConnell cut him off.

"No way, Jack," he said. "There's no way I'd ride out of here and leave you."

"You could get the women to safety, Skins," Pike said, "and come back for me."

"Come back, sure," McConnell said. "By the time I got back you'd be long dead and scalped.

167

Your 'head' that 'touches-the-sky' would be hanging on some brave's belt. No sir."

"I would not leave, either," Bright Deer said.

Betsy felt compelled to add, "Me, too," although she wasn't sure anyone even heard her.

"Well, what the hell was he doing asking about me if he's not going to go on talking?" Pike asked.

"Maybe if we just wait, we'll find out," McConnell said.

"They're circling us, you know," Pike said.

"I know," McConnell said.

"I did not hear them," Bright Deer said, frowning. It bothered her that they might have heard something that she had not.

"We don't have to hear them," McConnell said, "to know that they're there. It makes sense. It's probably also why they're not answering right now. They're waiting until they're all in position."

"Well," Pike said, "at least with our back to this wall, they can't get behind us."

There was a small overhang above them, so they were also safe from attack from above. Neither were they in any real danger from either side, since there were rocks all around them.

"We'd be pretty safe right here if we were just gonna wait," McConnell said. "If *they* were just gonna wait, but they ain't."

"No," Pike said, "they'll rush us sooner or later—unless I can get somebody's attention . . ."

"About what?" Betsy asked.

McConnell wondered, too, what had suddenly come to his friend's mind.

"Hello out there!" Pike called.

No answer.

"This is Pike!" the big man called. "Why were you asking about me?"

The silence went on so long he thought there would be no reply, but then the same voice answered.

"I want to know who I am killing," it said.

"You've been chasing us all this time without knowing who we were?" Pike asked. "I can't believe that."

"I hoped it was you," the voice said.

"Why?"

"You are a great warrior," the voice said. "It will bring much honor to kill you."

Now Pike had what he wanted.

"And who are you?"

No answer.

"I would like to know who is trying to kill me."

"I am Small Bear."

"Well, Small Bear, you're not going to kill me from hiding," he called back. "It will honor no one if you kill me from hiding, or through greater numbers. It would only bring you honor if you killed me yourself, hand-to-hand and face to face."

He hoped he wasn't going too fast for the brave's limited command of English.

"What are you doin' now?" McConnell said.

169

"That must be the leader talking," Pike said. "Maybe I can get him to come out and face me alone."

"And then after you kill him, the others kill us," McConnell said.

"Maybe," Pike said, "and maybe they'll just wait for the others to catch up. Or maybe the diversion will allow you to get away."

Suddenly, they heard their horses, and McConnell looked directly at Pike.

"On foot?"

"They have our horses?" Betsy asked.

Pike looked at her and said, "It was only a matter of time." He looked at McConnell and said, "If they don't move them, we may still have a chance. All I've got to do is get their leader to accept my challenge."

"Let's just hope he has enough courage to accept," McConnell said.

"Or honor," Bright Deer said.

"Or stupidity," Pike added.

Small Bear had kept two braves with him and sent the others to different positions. Now one of those braves returned with news.

"We have their animals," the brave said.

"Good," Small Bear said. "Do not move them. Just stay with them."

The brave nodded and moved away again.

"Will you accept his challenge?" one of the remaining braves asked Small Bear.

Small Bear gave the man a withering look and said, "Of course I will, and then I will kill He-Whose-Head-Touches-the-Sky with my bare hands."

"That will bring you much honor," the brave said.

"First," Small Bear said, "we will let them think a while."

Not too long, he thought, not long enough for Dark Moon to catch up, but long enough to worry about it.

"He's not gonna go for it," McConnell said, shaking his head.

"He must," Bright Deer said, "or lose face in front of the others."

"He's not Crow," Pike said.

"It does not matter," she said. "The Blackfeet are as prideful as the Crow."

"Or the Snake, for that matter," McConnell said, "or the Nez Perce, or any of them."

"What about white men?" Betsy asked. "Don't forget white men. They can be as prideful, or stubborn, as any Indian."

"Present company excepted, of course?" Pike said, looking at her.

Betsy looked back at him, but did not reply.

"Pike!"

They all looked up at the sound of the voice. It had been half an hour, or more, since they had last heard it. It commanded all of their attention.

"I'm still here."

"I am Small Bear." Had the Indian forgotten that he'd said that before, or did he just like the sound of his own name?

"What do you want, Small Bear?"

"You have challenged me."

Pike remained silent.

"I accept your challenge," Small Bear said.

"Good," Pike said. "Step out where I can see you."

"You must step out first."

"Don't . . ." Betsy said.

"One of us has to," Pike said, looking at her. "Besides, this'll show you that whites aren't *always* stubborn, huh?" He held his rifle out to Betsy and asked, "Can you use this?"

"I can use it," she said, taking it from him.

"There's always a chance they're just trying to lure me out into the open to cut down the odds," Pike said. "If they cut me down, I'll expect the rest of you to do me proud. Right?"

"We will avenge you," Bright Deer said.

"Do what you can to get *away,*" Pike said. "Understand? Skins?"

"If it comes down to gettin' away or gettin' re-

172

venge," McConnell said, "you know which one I'll do."

"I'm counting on you," Pike said, and then added to himself, I think.

"Small Bear?" he called.

"I am here."

"I'm coming out."

"Then come . . ."

One of the braves with Small Bear said, "I could kill him easily now."

"No," Small Bear said, "not unless the others try to interfere. If something goes wrong, kill him instantly. Understood?"

The two braves with him nodded. He knew the others would do nothing until he or these two braves did.

"We understand."

Small Bear nodded to them, and stood up.

Pike stepped out into the open, hesitated, then took a few steps to put some room between him and the others.

"I'm here," he called, spreading his arms. "Where are you, Small Bear?"

There was a long moment of silence during which he felt the tension between his shoulders, and then he saw the Indian stand.

"I am here, white man," Small Bear said.

The brave advanced a few feet, and the two men studied each other.

Small Bear was in his early thirties, not a strapping specimen but solid nonetheless. It would be no small matter to overcome him, even with Pike's size advantage. He knew that the advantage in speed would go to the brave.

Small Bear studied Pike intently. Since this was his first good look up close at He-Whose-Head-Touches-the-Sky, he wanted to study his opponent well. He was by far the biggest man—Indian *or* white—that Small Bear had ever seen, but the Blackfoot brave had enough confidence in himself so that he wasn't intimidated. *Impressed,* yes, but not intimidated.

"How do we do this?" Pike asked.

"You have a knife?" Small Bear asked.

"Yes."

Small Bear produced his, made some motions in the air with it and said, "Knives, then."

Pike took his knife out and said to Small Bear, "Before we do this, if I win, my friends go free, right?"

"We did not make that bargain," Small Bear said, shaking his head.

"I'm making it now."

Small Bear shrugged and said, "That will be up to my comrades."

174

Sonofabitch, Pike thought.

"Small Bear—"

"Defend yourself, white man," Small Bear said. "I am going to cut out your heart and eat it."

If you do, Pike thought, I hope you choke on it.

CHAPTER TWENTY-ONE

The two men seemed frozen in time for the moment while the others on both sides watched them.

Small Bear's braves were watching his every move, waiting for him to cut out the heart of the large white man and take a bite from it.

Bright Deer and Betsy kept their eyes on Pike, waiting for him to make a move on Small Bear.

McConnell was the only one who wasn't watching either Small Bear or Pike. He was looking around to see where the other Indians were. Small Bear seemed to have deployed his men around them, in a semi-circle. Since their backs were literally up against a stone wall, the braves couldn't *surround* them, but they had done their best to hem them in. So while the others watched the action, McConnell located each of the braves and made up his mind which of them he would go after first when the time came. By his best count, including Small Bear, they had at least eight braves to deal with.

That done, he then turned his attention to Pike

and Small Bear who, after sizing each other up, seemed prepared to finally engage each other in combat.

Pike watched Small Bear's eyes, while peripherally eyeing the man's shoulders. When the man decided to move, he'd give it away either by some movement of the eyes, or a hunching of his shoulders. By the same token, he knew that he'd never be able to move on this Indian brave without giving himself away beforehand. He chose to wait for Small Bear to make the first move, which the smaller, younger man eventually did.

Small Bear's eyes moved a split second before he did, and he feinted in towards Pike with his knife. As Pike moved back, Small Bear stopped, then suddenly *darted* forward. He lashed out with his knife and managed to cut through the front of Pike's shirt. Pike felt the blade also cut his flesh, and his shirt began to soak up blood, but he ignored it while mentally tipping his hat to Small Bear. He had paid for it with a bit of flesh, but he had learned something about the man. He was *fast,* and Pike respected that. Now he had to teach the brave something about himself, and make *him* respect the white man.

When the knife bit into Pike's abdomen, Betsy

177

flinched and thought she even felt Bright Deer do the same. McConnell did not react—at least not so that the two women could notice.

"He's hurt!" Betsy said aloud, squeezing McConnell's arm.

"No," McConnell said, "he's not hurt. That will just serve to wake him up."

"But he's bleeding—"

"Betsy," McConnell said, "look over there."

"Where?"

Without pointing he said, "There, over my right shoulder."

She tore her eyes away from Pike and Small Bear, who were now circling each other, and looked over McConnell's shoulder.

"What do you see?" he asked.

"Two braves."

"Keep your eyes on them," he said, "without letting them know you're keeping your eyes on them. Can you do that?"

"But Pike—"

"Never mind what's happening with Pike," McConnell said.

"But if he loses—"

"No matter who wins or loses," McConnell said, "what's important is what happens afterward, and if we're gonna stay alive, we have to be ready. Hold onto that rifle and keep your eyes on those two braves."

"All right," she said. She was holding the rifle

that Pike had given her, and now tightened her grip on it. She wanted very badly to turn her head to see what Pike was doing, but now she couldn't take her eyes off the two braves she was looking at over Skins McConnell's shoulder.

Small Bear feinted towards Pike a couple of more times, but Pike did not commit to a definite move. He feinted *back* in return, but never stopped moving.

"You are a patient fighter, white man," Small Bear said.

"As are you, my friend," Pike said.

"We might be here a very long time, since we are both patient."

"At least until the end," Pike said, and then he got an idea. "Or," he added, "until the rest of your braves arrive, with your leader."

The look on Small Bear's face told Pike that he had guessed correctly. Small Bear did not want the others to catch up *before* he was finished, *before* he could kill Pike, and the others. Small Bear wanted to do this on his own, and now that Pike had reminded him that there were more braves on the way, Small Bear threw patience—and with it caution—to the wind.

"I am going to kill you myself, He-Whose-Head-Touches-the-Sky," Small Bear said. "I will not share that pleasure with *anyone*."

"Not even your leader?"

"My *leader*," Small Bear said with disgust. "Dark Moon is a false leader, and I will show *everyone* who the real leader should be."

Pike did not recognize the name Dark Moon, but then he didn't know the name of every Blackfoot warrior in the Rockies.

It was obvious that Small Bear did not think much of Dark Moon's leadership abilities. Judging from the decisions Pike had seen—especially with the fires that were set—the man may have been right. Providing Pike and the others could come out of *this* particular predicament alive, that might be a valuable piece of information.

"You'd better kill me quickly, Small Bear," Pike said, actually taunting the man, "before Dark Moon comes and spoils it for you."

"Don't worry, white man," Small Bear said with a vicious grin, "I intend to kill you quickly. I would *like* to do it slowly, but you are a brave man, so I will not make you suffer."

"Gee," Pike said, "I really appreciate that, Small Bear. Come ahead."

"You are big, white man," Small Bear said, "and strong . . ."

"Yeah . . ." Pike said, waiting for the man to get to the point.

"But I am a warrior!"

"What does that mean?"

"I am a *warrior*," Small Bear said again, "a

180

Blackfoot warrior, worth any five white men."

"Well, come ahead, then, Small Bear," Pike said, "because I'm just one white man standing here waiting for you, waiting to prove to you what an old squaw's tale that is."

"Prepare to die, white man," Small Bear said, "and see if you can die like a warrior!"

"Bright Deer," McConnell said.

"Yes."

"Turn your head to the right, just a little."

She did as she was told, reluctantly.

"Do you see them?"

She frowned, then took her eyes away from Pike and Small Bear and saw what McConnell was talking about.

"Two braves," she said.

"Right," he said. "Keep your eyes on them and be ready with the pistol."

"To give it to him?"

"To use it yourself," McConnell said. "After Pike kills Small Bear, there won't be time to get a gun to him. You're gonna have to use it yourself."

"What do you mean, *when* Pike kills Small Bear?" Betsy asked. "How do you know Small Bear won't kill Pike?"

"I know Pike," McConnell said. "He'd never let anyone kill him while he thought two women were watching."

Of course, McConnell knew that Pike had no such vanity. He was simply trying to soothe the women's fears — and possibly his own, as well.

Small Bear charged Pike, and the big man put his arms straight out to ward the charge off. Pike's arms were corded with thick muscles, but it was still a jolt when the smaller man charged into him. The force of Small Bear's charge actually forced Pike back a couple of steps, but he then managed to deflect the man away from him. He turned to move on Small Bear, expecting the man to be off balance, which was not the case. The Blackfoot brave recovered his balance with remarkable speed, and had Pike committed to charging *him* at that point, the man would have been ready for him and would probably have gutted him there and then.

"Come, white man," Small Bear said, "let us bring this to an end."

"Oh, I don't know," Pike said. "I sort of thought I wouldn't mind waiting for Dark Moon to get here. Maybe he'd like to watch."

Small Bear bellowed like a wounded bear and charged Pike once more. Again, Pike readied himself for the impact, but it never came. As Small Bear charged he suddenly fell — but he *hadn't* fallen. He had dropped to the ground, and he *kicked* Pike's feet out from under him. Unprepared for the quickness of the man's move, Pike felt himself falling, and in that instant felt helpless, and open.

Small Bear, with swiftness that was by now characteristic, lunged with the knife, and Pike felt the blade bite into his left forearm, drawing blood again.

"Damn!" McConnell swore as more of Pike's blood stained the ground.

"What happened?" Betsy asked.

"Never mind," McConnell said. "Keep your eyes on your men."

"What is happening?" Bright Deer asked.

"They're still dancin' around each other," McConnell lied. "Just be ready, ladies. It shouldn't take much longer now."

He *hoped* it wouldn't take much longer, and he hoped that the outcome would be in their favor.

And he hoped that when all hell broke loose, everyone would be able to do their part.

"Ha!" Small Bear laughed, but as he was about to stab again Pike was suddenly gone. The big man had gotten to his feet again and backed off. It was then that Small Bear realized that Pike was faster than a man his size should be, Indian *or* white man.

Pike was bleeding now from the wound to his

abdomen and the wound in his left arm. He knew that if Small Bear wanted to drag this out, he would slowly lose strength as he lost blood. Luckily, Small Bear was in a hurry, and knowing *that* was Pike's advantage.

"Come on, Small Bear," Pike said. He held his arm out so that his blood fell to the ground in a pool. "I've got plenty of blood left."

"Do you want me to take you in pieces, white man?" Small Bear asked.

"Just take me, Small Bear," Pike said, "and stop talking about it. Goddamn, I swear you're trying to *talk* me to death."

Small Bear narrowed his eyes, and Pike could swear he heard the man growl deep in his throat like an animal—and then he *sprang* like an animal. With the speed of a mountain cat, Small Bear was almost on him. At the very last moment Small Bear's moccasined right foot came down on a small pool Pike's blood had left in the ground. The foot went out from beneath him just enough to throw him off balance for an instant. That instant was all Pike needed. Small Bear was leaning forward slightly as a result of the slip, and Pike brought his knife up and drove it into the man's belly.

Small Bear screamed!

CHAPTER TWENTY-TWO

The scream echoed for miles. . . .

When Dark Moon heard the scream, he knew that it was Small Bear. Of course, he didn't recognize the voice, because that was kind of hard to do when someone was screaming, but *instinctively* he knew that Small Bear had found He-Whose-Head-Touches-the-Sky, and had paid the ultimate price.

He looked around at his other braves and saw the confusion in their faces. *They* had no idea who was screaming, but after a few moments the looks on their faces became smug as they *assumed* that whoever was screaming was a white man.

Dark Moon would never tell them that they were wrong.

When Small Bear screamed, Skins McConnell said to the women, "Get ready!"

Both women looked at the two braves who were

their responsibility, but the Indians seemed to be frozen in place, undecided as to what they were supposed to do.

So, too, were the other braves who were watching the fight.

As Small Bear fell to the ground, Pike did not waste any time. He knew that the other braves would have a few seconds of indecision, and he wanted to take advantage of that. He pulled his knife free of Small Bear's body and charged the indecisive braves.

McConnell was ready, but he couldn't afford to leave the women alone.

"Fire!" he said to them.

"But . . . they're not moving," Betsy said.

McConnell's reply was cut off as Bright Deer fired her gun. McConnell took a quick look and saw that she had hit one of the braves. As he fell the other brave leaped into action and charged. McConnell raised his rifle and shot the man before he took two steps.

On the other side, Betsy closed her eyes and fired, missing entirely. McConnell was ready for that, too, though. He leaped from cover and charged the two braves just as they started to move. He hit one of them so hard in the face with his rifle stock that the brave's nose was smashed flat. He swung the rifle again and hit the other man with the barrel. The brave's forehead split, and he went down. McConnell dropped his rifle and, without hesitation, produced his knife and slit the throats of both men.

He turned then to go to Pike's aid, but saw that his big friend had the situation well in hand. He was standing, and three braves were lying on the ground. If there were any others, they had run off.

He approached Pike and saw that, although his friend was bleeding from several nicks and cuts, he was in pretty good shape.

"The plan worked," McConnell said, looking around.

The two women stepped from cover and approached the two men.

"Are you all right?" Betsy asked Pike.

"I'm fine," Pike said. He was breathing heavily, but his tone was steady.

"Get him patched up," McConnell told the two women. "I'll go and see how many horses I can find."

"Reload first," Pike said to all of them, which was excellent advice.

Betsy reloaded Pike's rifle, and he held it across his knees while the two women patched his wounds. McConnell, having reloaded, went to find some horses.

At the sound of the shots Dark Moon called his braves to a halt. They sat their horses and listened, counting the shots. Once again, the braves were confused as to what was going on, but Dark Moon knew that the shots meant that Small Bear's braves were paying the price for following Small Bear.

Their forces were now somewhat depleted, but should still be enough to run down and finish the two white men, and the two women with them — providing the leadership was solid. Without Small Bear questioning his every move, it wouldn't be long before they caught up to the whites. Maybe along the way they would find the bodies of Small Bear and his braves. That would teach *these* braves to follow the proven leader if they wanted to succeed.

Pike's wounds had been cleaned and bound as best they could by the time McConnell returned to the clearing with three horses. Two of them were Indian ponies; the other was the horse Pike had been riding.

"Could only find one of ours," he said. "We'll have to make do."

"I'll share the pony with Bright Deer," Pike said. "You take the other, and let Betsy ride my horse.

"Agreed," McConnell said.

Betsy looked as if she wanted to protest the preferential treatment, but in the end she was too tired to argue. Besides, she realized that it made sense. She was probably the only one of the four of them who hadn't ridden bareback before.

"We'd better get moving," McConnell said. "Dark Moon is bound to have heard everything that went on."

"Maybe he'll think we're dead," Betsy said, hopefully. "Maybe he'll just go away."

The others did not bother to look at her. She knew she was wrong without being told.

"Come on, Betsy," McConnell said. He laced his hands together and held them out to her. "Up you go."

She stepped into his man-made stirrup and swung onto the back of Pike's horse.

Pike mounted, and reached down to pull Bright Deer up behind him. McConnell mounted up, and then turned to look behind them.

"Forget it," Pike said. "From now on we stay together. It'll be safer that way."

McConnell hesitated, then said, "All right, I agree. Let's ride."

"Where?" Betsy asked. "Where do we ride to?"

"We're going to have to find Nathan Wynan's camp," Pike said. "His is probably the only force large enough to withstand what's left of the Indians."

"What do you think happened to the others?" Betsy asked. "Joe Gall, and the others . . ."

Pike and McConnell exchanged a glance that Betsy caught.

"They're dead, aren't they?" she asked. "As dead as my husband."

"Maybe," McConnell said, "some of them got away; maybe some of them made it to Wynan's camp by now."

"Well," Pike said, "there's only one way to find out, isn't there?"

"We've got to get to his camp ourselves, McConnell said. "He'll have enough men with him to keep these braves from following us."

"What then?" Bright Deer asked.

Pike looked at her and said, "We'll decide that when the time comes. First we *get* to safety, and then we decide what to do after that."

"Come on," McConnell said, looking down at the dead braves. "We've stayed around here long enough. The others will be here soon."

Pike looked at Betsy and Bright Deer, but Betsy knew that his remark was directed more to her than to the Indian woman.

"From here on in we don't stop to rest," he said. "We ride until either we drop, or the horses do. Understood?"

Bright Deer nodded, and Betsy said, "Yes."

"And if the horses drop first," McConnell added, "we walk."

"If we end up on foot," Betsy said, "they'll catch up to us."

"Don't worry," McConnell said, looking her right in the eyes. "I won't let them take you."

She stared back at him. She knew full well what he meant. He would put a ball into her brain before he'd let the Indians take her or him or Pike. They might not do the same for Bright Deer. She was Crow, and the Blackfeet would probably just kill her. Betsy, however, was white, and the Blackfeet would make good use of her before they killed her — *if* they even decided to kill her. Actually, if they did kill her, they'd probably be doing her a favor.

"I understand," she said.

McConnell nodded and looked at Pike, who also nodded. Bright Deer's face was impassive, but McConnell knew that they *all* understood.

Later, Dark Moon and his braves rode into the clearing where Small Bear and the other braves lay dead.

Dark Moon dismounted and checked the body of Small Bear, just to make sure that the man was dead. The other braves milled about, checking their fallen comrades, all of whom were dead.

"Two white men could not have done this," one brave said.

"There must have been more," another said

"There were only two," Dark Moon said, facing them.

"But how could that be?" the first brave asked. "These were Blackfeet warriors!"

"Small Bear was not a true leader," Dark Moon said. "He was foolish, and his foolishness was his undoing. The others, they simply died with him."

"Then what will we do?" the brave asked.

"We will do what he should have done," Dark Moon. "We will hunt them down and kill them, and we will make no foolish mistakes. If you trust me, and follow me, we will make no mistakes."

The braves exchanged glances all the way around, and then the first brave spoke.

"You are our leader, Dark Moon," he said. "We will follow you."

"Good," Dark Moon said, "good. We will go. Later, we will return for our fallen brothers."

This was as good as a test. The braves exchanged glances again, knowing that in their absence several different kinds of animals might come and feed on the carcasses of their brothers. If they followed him, even knowing this, then he knew they would do whatever he commanded them to do.

"You lead, Dark Moon," the brave said, "and we will follow."

"Then we go," Dark Moon said, "now."

CHAPTER TWENTY-THREE

Nathan Wynan woke that morning with a feeling of dread. That was odd, because he was awakened by the fact that his woman, Alicia, was crouched down between his legs, her mouth avidly working on him, bringing him awake *and* ready at the same time. When his penis was a rigid pole, standing straight up, she raised her wide hips and brought herself down on him, taking him inside of her. He slid his hands beneath her wonderfully wide buttocks, enjoying the feel of her smooth skin against his calloused palms. Alicia was a big woman by anyone's standards, with breasts and buttocks that were full and solid, and when she began to bounce on him, her weight jarred him. Wynan, *not* a big man, did not mind. Though not very large himself, he was solidly built and strong enough to withstand the pummelling his body would take from Alicia in this position. Later, he would flip her over, mount her and take her that way, and it would only be after that that he would once again think of his feeling of dread as he awakened. . . .

* * *

When the riders came into camp, Nathan Wynan knew something was wrong. As they came closer, he noticed that they had a body slung across a horse, and he rushed forward to meet them. They were his men, who had gone out just hours before to check their traps. Their premature return was a sure signal of trouble.

"What's wrong?" Wynan asked.

"It's Joe Gall," one of the men said. His name was Forester, and he had led the party of five out of camp that morning.

"Is he dead?" Wynan asked.

"No," Forester said, then added, "not yet. He's pretty damned frozen, though."

"What the hell happened?" Wynan asked.

"Don't know," Forester said. "We ain't been able to ask him."

"Get him down and into one of the tents. I'll have Alicia take a look at him."

Forester nodded. He turned and relayed the order to two of his men. They dismounted, picked Joe Gall up off his horse and carried him to a tent.

Forester dismounted and stood next to Wynan, handing his reins to one of the other men.

"Did you see any sign of anyone else?" Wynan asked.

"No," Forester said, "nobody. He looks like he's come a long way, Nathan."

194

"He had a lot of people with him," Wynan said.

"They could have been attacked," Forester said. "If that's the case, they could be scattered to the four winds."

Wynan rubbed his hand over his face.

"Dead," he said, "a lot of them could be dead, others in the same condition he's in."

"It would have to have been a large war party," Forester said. "Blackfeet, Snake—"

"Blackfeet," Wynan said. "It had to be."

"What do we do, Nathan?" Forester asked. "We can't leave them out there."

Wynan thought a moment, then said, "Let's see if we can bring him around and ask him some questions. Before we go rushing out there, we should have some idea what we're gonna face."

"All right," Forester said, "but if we have to go out and take a look, I volunteer. I had some friends in Gall's group."

"We all had friends with him, Lee," Wynan said. "That's no reason to go off half-cocked, right?"

"You're right, Nathan," Lee Forester said, "you're right."

"Let's see how Alicia's doin'," Wynan said.

"Right."

They had Joe Gall packed with blankets, trying to warm him up. He wasn't conscious, or they would have been feeding him soup.

"Alicia?" Wynan asked.

There were two other women in the tent with her. She said something to one of them, then joined Wynan outside the tent.

"He's almost frozen solid, Nathan," she said. "I . . . I don't see how we can save his feet . . . he may lose some of his fingers . . . and that's if we can manage to keep him alive."

"I need to talk to him, Allie," he said.

"Nathan," she said, "I haven't been able to wake him up, yet."

"Do your best, honey," he said. "There were a lot of people out there with him. We need to know what happened to them."

"I understand," she said. "I'll do my best. Hell, I'll get under the blankets with him if it comes to that."

"Hell," Wynan said, trying to lighten the mood, "*that* would sure raise the dead, wouldn't it?"

"Nathan," she said, sternly. She kissed his cheek and went back into the tent.

Wynan turned to find Forester approaching him.

"How is he?" Forester asked.

"Unconscious."

"Nathan, I've got twenty volunteers ready to go," Forester said. "I don't think we can afford to wait."

"Lee—"

"Hear me out," Forester said, "We'll go out and take a look. When he wakes up and you get some

196

information out of him, send a rider after us with it."

Wynan hesitated, then said, "I don't know. I can't send men out there without knowing—"

"You're not sending us," Forester reminded him. "We're going on our own. Nathan, we've got to do *something*. We can't just sit here."

"Everyone feels the same?" Wynan asked.

"Ask them," Forester said. "Ask them yourself."

Wynan rubbed his hand over his face again, then ran his hands through his hair.

"All right, Lee," he said, finally. "Get your men ready, but don't ride out until I say so. All right?"

"Agreed, Nathan," Forester said, "and thanks."

"Yeah," Wynan said to the man's retreating back, "thank me when you're all back safe."

While Pike, McConnell and the women were involved in their battle in the clearing, most of the horses must have scattered good and wide, because they rode half the day without coming across any of them. Still, the Indian ponies they had were a hearty stock. Pike's horse was the only question mark, as it had been through a lot, already.

Pike kept his eyes on the horse, watching for a wrong step. He didn't want the animal going down on top of Betsy. It might not have been such a good idea to give her the saddle horse, after all.

Pike's sharp eyes caught something in the horse's stride, and he called out for them to stop.

"What is it?" McConnell asked.

"Get Betsy off that horse," Pike said, dropping down from his pony.

McConnell got to her first and helped her down. Pike leaned over the horse and ran his hands over him. He could feel the weakness in the animal's legs, a weakness he thought he had detected while watching it. He could have sworn that the horse's front legs were shaking every few steps, and now he knew he was right.

"He did feel a little shaky," Betsy said.

"He's gone as far as he's going to go," Pike said, patting the animal's neck. "Let's get this saddle off him and send him on his way."

"What will you do now?" she asked. "Saddle one of the ponies?"

"I don't think so," Pike said, stripping the saddle from the animal's back. "I think you'll just have to ride double with Skins."

He dropped the saddle to the ground, pulled the blanket off the horse's back, and then slapped the animal in the rump. It trotted off shakily.

"Will it survive?" Betsy asked.

"I don't know," Pike said.

McConnell mounted up again, and Pike helped Betsy climb up behind him. He walked to his own pony then and took a moment to run his hands up and down the animal's legs. It still felt strong and

198

steady, but how long could even the hearty Indians pony carry double weight without rest?

He mounted up in front of Bright Deer, and she put her arms around his waist.

"I could walk," she said in his ear.

"We may all be walking soon," he said to her. "Let's just ride as long and as far as we can."

She tightened her arms around him, and they started off again, riding behind McConnell and Betsy.

"It'll be dark soon," Forester said to Wynan. "I know," Wynan said. "Maybe you should wait until morning."

"We'd like to get out there now, and use what daylight we have left," Forester said. "We'll take some supplies and camp when it gets dark. Gall may revive during the night, and you can send a rider to find us."

Wynan hated sending them out there, but he decided that they had waited as long as they dared.

"Look," he said, "there's a good chance that if there are any of his people left, they're probably in the same shape he is."

"If we can get them back here—"

"Look," Wynan said, "Lee, just don't take any unnecessary chances, all right? There's no point in all of you ending up like him, all right?"

Forester knew that Gall was on the verge of losing his feet, and most of his fingers to frostbite, and he had no intention of ending up the same way. He'd rather be dead than chewed up by the cold that way.

"Don't worry, Nathan," he said. "We'll be back."

"You'd better be," Wynan said, clapping him on the shoulder. "I need you here."

Forester nodded and went to tell his men that they were moving out.

Of course, when Pike had told Betsy and Bright Deer that they wouldn't be stopping, he had *meant* that they wouldn't stop until dark. Travelling in the dark was just too risky. A misstep by one of the horses, and they could end up with a broken arm, or leg . . . or neck.

"A cold camp?" McConnell said to Pike.

"No," Pike said. "I thought about that. We'll just end up dying before morning."

"They'll find us if we build a fire," Betsy said.

Pike looked at her.

"I'd rather die quick, in a battle, then freeze to death slowly. How about you?"

She didn't answer. She knew that *she* wouldn't be dying in battle. Pike or McConnell would see to it that she was dead long before that possibility.

"Whatever you say," she said.

They found an outcropping of rock and decided to build their fire behind it.

"Maybe they won't see it," Pike said, but he knew as well as McConnell *and* Bright Deer that the Blackfeet would *smell* the campfire. None of them said that to Betsy, though. No point, really.

Once the fire was built they huddled closely around it, Pike and Bright Deer sharing a blanket *and* body warmth while McConnell and Betsy did the same. Pike and McConnell kept their rifles close by.

"You know," McConnell said, "if even one person — Gall or *somebody* — got through to Wynan's camp, they might be looking for us right now."

"Us?" Betsy said.

"Well, anybody," McConnell said. "Survivors. As it turns out, that's us."

"Maybe we'll run into them tomorrow," Pike said.

"Jesus, I hope so," Betsy said.

Bright Deer had her hands underneath Pike's shirt, seeking the warmth of his flesh for her cold hands. In spite of their situation, he found himself responding to the nearness of her, the feel of her hips pressed solidly to his, her hands on his skin.

Well, he thought, at least my *crotch* is warm.

CHAPTER TWENTY-FOUR

When Nathan Wynan was told that Joe Gall had died, he started shaking his head.

"Did he say anything?" he asked Alicia.

"He said a few things, Nathan," Alicia said. "He never really finished a sentence, but mentioned some names."

"What names?"

"He said 'Pike' and he said 'Skins.' That would be Jack Pike, wouldn't it, Nathan?"

"I don't know any other Pike," Wynan said.

"And Skins?"

"Skins McConnell," Wynan said. "He usually rides with Pike."

"I guess he was trying to tell us that Pike and McConnell are out there," Alicia said.

Wynan rubbed his jaw.

"I can't see Pike and McConnell hooking up with Gall," he said. "Joe was a good man, but I never did think he had what it took to be a leader."

"Maybe it was the other way around," Alicia said.

"What do you mean?"

"Maybe they didn't hook up with him, maybe *he* hooked up with *them*."

Wynan rubbed his beard.

"That's a possibility, I guess," he admitted. "In fact, it makes more damn sense."

"Nate," she said, "what about that fire we saw earlier this week?"

"I remember," Nathan said.

"That could have been at Gall's camp," she said. "They probably got attacked by Indians."

"If that's the case, there's got to be more people out there than just Pike and McConnell," Wynan said.

Alicia studied Wynan for a long moment and then said, "You would hope that there are more survivors than just them."

"Alicia, did he say anything else?"

"He mumbled a lot," she said. "I think he said something about women."

"Maybe Pike and McConnell have some women with them," Wynan said. "Did Gall have any women with him in his camp?"

"I think Betsy Walters was with him," she said. "I mean, with her husband. And Alice Kincaid."

"Didn't Hobbs have a woman with him?" Wynan asked.

"That's right," Alicia said, "a Crow woman."

"Any others?"

She frowned and said, "Not that I can think of right now."

"Okay," he said, taking a deep breath, "let's get Gall buried, and then send someone out to find Forester and tell him what we know."

"Which isn't much," Alicia said.

"It sure ain't," Wynan agreed, shaking his head. "Ain't much, at all."

Pike woke the others so they could benefit from the last few minutes that the fire would be lit. They all had coffee, and then he kicked the fire out.

"I'm worried about Betsy," McConnell said as they saw to the horses.

"What about her?"

"She's gettin' weak," McConnell said. "I don't know how much longer she can go on."

"She'll go on as long as the rest of us do," Pike said, with conviction.

"Pike," McConnell said, "maybe you better think about goin' on ahead with Bright Deer."

"Forget it."

"No, I'm serious—"

"So am I," Pike said. "We're not leaving you and Betsy behind."

"She's gonna slow us down, Jack," McConnell said. "You know that."

"Yeah, I know it."

"It don't make sense for all of us to die."

"Okay," Pike said, facing his friend, "I'll tell you what. The three of us will go on without her and leave her behind."

"What?" McConnell said, looking shocked. "You can't be serious. I can't leave her behind like that."

"Right," Pike said, "then don't ask me to leave you behind, or her. Okay?"

McConnell stared at Pike for a few seconds, and then shrugged and said, "Okay, okay, I get your point."

"What's going on here?" Betsy asked, coming up behind them.

McConnell looked at her and said, "We were discussin' strategy."

"And what did you come up with?" she asked.

Pike looked at her this time and said, "We decided that we better run like hell."

"Well," Betsy said, "I'm ready." But both men could see that she was far from ready. She was drawn and haggard, and her every movement betrayed her exhaustion.

Bright Deer came up on them then and said, "Are we leaving?"

"Right now," Pike said.

They mounted up and rode out of camp with Betsy clinging to McConnell from behind. He could feel the lack of strength in her arms as they encircled his waist.

"You were talking about me, weren't you?" she asked after they had ridden a while.

"What?"

"You and Pike, this morning," she said. "You were talking about me, weren't you?"

"We were talking about everything, Betsy," he said. "You included."

"You should leave me behind," she said.

"Don't be silly."

"I'm tired, Skins."

"We're all tired."

"No, you know what I mean," she said. "I'm about played out. You and Pike can see it, even Bright Deer can see it. I'm gonna slow you all down."

"Betsy—"

"I'm gonna get you all killed," she said.

"Betsy," McConnell said, "I tried to get Pike and Bright Deer to go on ahead of us, but he refused."

"You should *all* go on ahead without me."

"Stop it," he said, harshly, putting his left hand on her arms. "We're not going to leave you behind, so just forget that talk, you hear?"

She hesitated, then said, "I hear."

She tightened her arms around him, but soon her grip loosened again. Every so often he would just put his hand on her arms to make sure that she was still holding on, and not just *hanging* on.

Up ahead Pike was talking to Bright Deer about the situation with Betsy.

"The Crow or the Blackfeet would just leave her behind," Bright Deer said.

"Any of the tribes would," Pike said. "Maybe

that's why we think we're more civilized than they are."

"Whites," Bright Deer said against his back.

"What does that mean?"

"It would make sense for you *and* Skins to leave me behind with Betsy and go for help. I could keep her alive until you got back."

"If we got back," Pike said, "and if you could keep yourself alive, at the same time."

"I am fine."

There *was* no trace of fatigue in the Crow woman, but Pike was feeling the strain himself, and figured that she surely must by now, as well.

"I know you are," he said, patting her hands that were clasped around his waist.

Dark Moon looked down at the dead fire and knew they were just hours behind the whites, now.

"It will not be long now," he said to his men. "They are just ahead."

Privately, some of the braves thought that the hunt had gone on long enough already. The attack on the camp had gone badly, and they had lost Small Bear and many of their braves to these white men. Some of them thought it might be time to go back, and forget about He-Whose-Head-Touches-the-Sky—who couldn't be killed, anyway!

Dark Moon was aware of the discontent of some of his braves, but he had come too far now to even think about giving up. His only redemption now was to take Pike, the legend, and to show everyone that he *could* be killed, that even a legend — like He-Whose-Head-Touches-the-Sky — could be killed — which would make the warrior who killed him a legend, as well.

Dark Moon looked around him at the faces of his braves. Many of them looked away, and he knew what was in their minds and their hearts. That would change, though. Once they caught up to the whites, and he killed Pike, all of that would change.

CHAPTER TWENTY-FIVE

When Lee Forester and his men broke camp that morning, Forester was deep in thought. He and the others had been all gung ho about riding out here to look for survivors, and Forester also remembered the big fire they had seen earlier in the week. It had been a long way off, and it didn't seem to make much sense then to go riding out half-cocked to see what had happened. By the same token, how much sense did it make to do it now?

It had been cold last night, away from Wynan's camp. Maybe they were just spoiled, having been part of a huge camp for so long, with warm food and fires, and some warm, willing women. Also, they had expected a rider from camp with some information, and so far no one had been forthcoming.

Forester looked around and wondered what the other men would think if he suggested now that they go back.

At that moment he *did* hear a rider approaching, as did the others. They all looked up and saw a lone man riding into their camp. They all recognized him as Tate Billings, from Wynan's camp.

Billings reined his horse and dismounted, approaching Forester.

"What's happened?" Forester asked.

"Gall died during the night," Billings said.

Forester looked around and saw that his men were doing the same, muttering and exchanging glances.

"Did he say anything?"

"He mentioned a couple of names," Billings said, "Pike and Skins. Nate figures he was talking about Jack Pike and Skins McConnell."

"I know Pike," Forester said, and some of the other men said they knew either Pike or McConnell.

"He figures they were with Gall," Billing said, and went on to explain what else Nathan Wynan was assuming. When Billings mentioned the fire, it made sense to Forester. Somehow, Gall, Pike, and McConnell had survived the fire attack on the camp. Billings also mentioned the possibility that Pike and McConnell might have some women with them, as well.

Forester remembered Betsy Walters from when she and her husband were in Wynan's camp. She was a sad-looking woman he had found attractive.

"What does Nate want us to do?" Forester asked.

"He said he's gonna leave that up to you, Lee," Billings said.

Forester nodded, and said to Billings, "All right, go on back, Tate."

"If you don't mind, Lee," Billings said, "I'd like to go along with you—that is, if you *are* still going to search for survivors."

"Are we?" Forester asked, looking around at his men.

To a man they all agreed that they were.

"We're goin' on," Forester said to Billings. "Let's get mounted up."

Wynan and Alicia were sitting at a fire in front of the tent they shared. Around them the camp was a bustle of activity, but she could see that her man's mind was somewhere else.

"You wish you were out there, don't you?" she asked. "Looking for them?"

"I know Pike," Wynan said. "I know him well. If there's any way in hell that he could survive, he would."

"But you'd like to help him?"

"Hell, yes," Wynan said.

"Nate, they're probably trying to find their way here," she suggested. "If they were with Gall, he would have told them about us."

"You're right."

"And you can't leave here," she said. "Your responsibility is to these people—"

"I know where my responsibilities are!" he snapped at her—and he was immediately sorry for it. "I'm sorry, Allie—"

"It's all right," she said, reaching out to touch his face. I understand. You're frustrated, and who else is there to yell at?"

"I should never yell at you," he said, taking her hand in his.

"They'll make it, Nate," she said. "Pike will make it, and if Forester and the others can help him, they will."

"I know," he said, squeezing her hand, "I know . . ."

"What else is bothering you?" she asked. "Gall?"

He looked at her and said, "What are you, woman, some kind of damned mind reader?"

"I can't read minds," she said, "but I can read yours. You blame yourself for Gall's death."

"Gall, and all the people who went with him," Wynan said.

"Why?" she asked. "They went with him willingly. No one forced them."

"I could have stopped them."

"How?"

"By stopping Gall," he said. "I could have kept Joe from going, and that would have kept the

212

others from going, as well. And they'd all be here and alive right now."

"Maybe," she said, "maybe . . ."

"No maybe about it," he said.

"That still don't make it your fault," she said. "You're a leader, Nate, but you're not anybody's father . . ."

He looked at her and said, "Don't you see, Allie? It's the same thing . . . it's the same *damned* thing!"

Never having been a leader—or a mother—she couldn't quite see how it was the same thing, but she loved and respected Nathan Wynan, and she could see that he was in pain. Did he really look at all these people as his children?

If McConnell hadn't caught her, Betsy would have fallen from her position behind him. He felt her hold on his slacken, and he reached behind him for her right away and caught her.

"Pike!" he shouted.

Pike heard him and wheeled his horse around. He saw what had happened and rode back. He dropped down from his pony and took hold of Betsy, easing her from the horse and holding her in his arms.

"I'm sorry . . ." Betsy said, her voice faint. "I'm sorry . . . I can't . . ."

McConnell dismounted, as did Bright Deer,

who took the pony from McConnell.

"Let me have her," McConnell said, taking Betsy from Pike.

Pike grabbed a blanket and spread it on the ground for McConnell to lay Betsy on. Bright Deer handed him another blanket, and he used this one to cover the fallen woman.

"She's barely conscious," McConnell said. He looked at Pike and said, "You don't have much of a choice now, do you?"

"Skins —"

"You and Bright Deer have to go on, Pike," McConnell said. "I'll stay here with Betsy and wait for you."

"But, Skins —

"Build me a fire," McConnell said, "leave me some supplies, and get the hell out of here!"

Pike looked across Betsy's still form at Bright Deer, who stared back at him boldly.

"I will stay with her," she said.

McConnell looked at Bright Deer and said, "No, I have to stay."

Pike was at a loss, and for the first time he was feeling fatigued — physically *and* mentally. What should he do? Leave McConnell behind with Betsy? Bright Deer? If he left the Crow woman behind with the white woman, how long would either of them last? And would McConnell fare any better? What if *he* stayed behind instead of one of them? How would that turn out?

"Pike!" McConnell said, and Pike realized that this was the third time his friend had called his name.

"What?"

"You' re wasting time," McConnell said, "precious time. Get going."

"Skins—"

"To tell you the truth, Pike," McConnell said, grabbing his friend's arm, "I'm about played out, too. I don't know how much longer I can keep this up. Pike, you're stronger than I am. Goddamn, man, you're a horse! Our only chance of gettin' out of this alive is for you to keep goin'—you and Bright Deer, both."

"No," Bright Deer said, "not me. I, too, am tired. Pike must go on alone. He will move faster like that."

"That's it then," McConnell said, looking at his friend. "Your outvoted, partner. We're *all* putting our lives in your hands."

"You sonofabitch," Pike said to his friend. "If you're dead when I get back, I'll never speak to you again."

McConnell grinned weakly and said, "I'll keep that in mind. Now get your big ass movin'."

Pike stood up, walked to his pony, and dropped what supplies they had onto the ground.

"Hey," McConnell said, "keep somethin' for yourself."

215

"I won't be needing it," Pike said, leaping astride the pony. I won't be stopping."

"Pike—"

"I'll be back soon, Skins," Pike promised. *"Real* soon."

CHAPTER TWENTY-SIX

After Pike left them, McConnell said to Bright Deer, "We're gonna need a fire, and you're gonna have to stay with her while I stand watch."

"I will build the fire," Bright Deer said.

"Good."

While she collected the makings of a fire, McConnell did his best to try and make Betsy comfortable. At one point her eyes fluttered open, and she looked up at him.

"Skins . . ."

"Take it easy, Betsy."

"What happened?"

"Your spirit is willing," he said, "but your body just gave out."

"Oh . . . I'm sorry . . ."

"Don't be sorry," he said. "I was about to quit, myself."

She closed her eyes then and said, weakly, "Liar."

McConnell wanted to tell her that he may have been exaggerating a little, but he certainly wasn't lying. It was his feeling that they were all very nearly played out, although Bright Deer was certainly giving no outward indication of it.

Once the Crow woman had the fire going, McConnell picked up his rifle and said, "I'm going to stand watch—not that it'll do much good. If they catch up to us now, we're as good as finished."

Bright Deer had Pike's Kentucky pistol on the ground near her.

"Bright Deer," he said, "if they do catch up to us, and I can't get to Betsy in time . . ."

Bright Deer looked at him and touched the pistol with her hand.

"I will take care of her," she promised.

He looked at her and said, "Thanks."

Pike knew he was punishing the pony beneath him by pushing the animal so hard, but he felt he had little choice. McConnell and the two women were in a position now where they would be virtually helpless if Dark Moon and his braves caught up to them.

Pike and McConnell had talked briefly about Dark Moon since they had heard the name from Small Bear. Neither of them had ever heard of him before, so they assumed that Dark Moon was probably a young warrior who was trying to establish himself as a leader among his people. Although they didn't know who he was, or what kind of man he was, it was very likely that he had a lot to prove. *That* meant there wasn't much chance that he'd give up the chase until he caught them.

Pike was still thinking about Dark Moon when he felt the pony either misstep, or simply stumble from exhaustion. He had time to throw himself clear before the animal fell heavily to the ground.

Pike gathered himself together and got to his feet. He walked over to where the pony was lying. The animal's eyes were open, and its sides were heaving as it fought to catch its breath. He checked it for injuries and found none. It was obvious that he had simply ridden the animal into the ground.

Pike stood, grabbed his rifle, and checked it for damage. Finding it in working condition, he walked to the horse, placed the barrel against the gallant animal's head, and pulled the trigger.

McConnell's head jerked up at the sound of the shot, and he was alert for any that might follow. When none did, he looked over at Bright Deer, who was sitting on the ground next to Betsy. The Crow woman had her chin up, listening intently for more shots. When none came, she looked over at McConnell.

The horse, McConnell thought. Pike had to shoot the horse. Even given time to reload, if Pike was in trouble he would have fired again by now. One single shot indicated a *necessity* for just one shot. If the horse were injured, or had simply run as far as it could run, Pike would put a bullet in its brain to put it out of its misery.

And that would put Pike on foot.

At the sound of the shot, Lee Forester called his men to a halt, and they all listened intently.

"One shot?" Billings said. "Why?"

"I don't know," Forester said. "Where did it come from, do you think?"

"It's hard to tell," Billings said, "what with the echo and all."

Forester looked around, to see if anyone else had an opinion. By the time they were all done speaking, he decided that they might as well continue on in the direction they were going.

Dark Moon heard the shot, as did his braves, but he did not halt their progress. He knew they were going in the right direction. It wouldn't be long now before they caught up with the fleeing whites. This whole thing would be over, and Dark Moon would have redeemed himself.

Pike's instinct was to run at full speed, but he knew that he'd run *himself* into the ground that way. He had to pace himself, running not for speed, but for distance and time. He had to run as far and as long as he had to in order to reach help. McConnell—and the two women—were counting on him.

"How is she?" McConnell called out to Bright Deer.

"Not good," the Crow woman said. "She needs food, and rest."

"We all do," McConnell said. Betsy, unfortunately, was the weakest of the four of them, and the first to succumb to exhaustion. All that meant was that the others—McConnell himself, Bright Deer, Pike—would eventually fall prey to it, as well.

Pike would probably be next, especially if he was on foot, now. He would run and run and run, and if he didn't run *into* anyone pretty soon—preferably some of Nathan Wynan's men—then he would probably run himself right into the ground.

McConnell frowned, looking at Bright Deer. Which one of them would last the longest, he wondered? He would like to think it would be him, since he was the man, but as Bright Deer was fond of telling Pike, he *was* a white man, and she *was* a Crow woman.

Who would be the last to keel over, he wondered?

And would they even have the chance to find out before they were overrun by the Blackfeet braves?

He turned his attention away from Bright Deer, on the lookout again for Dark Moon and his men. McConnell was determined that he would get off at least one shot at the leader, Dark Moon. Maybe, if he killed him, the others would turn and flee.

Sure. More than likely they'd simply ride him down, kill him, and then the women. Hopefully, Bright Deer would have time to put a ball in Betsy's brain, saving her from being used. It was then that McConnell realized that even if he *did* manage to use his one shot to kill Dark Moon, he'd be leaving Bright Deer at the mercy of the Blackfeet. That wouldn't be fair to her, would it? He was going to have to use that one shot on her, if he could, and then try to kill Dark Moon with his bare hands.

Shit, he thought, wiping his brow, is this what it's like to be delirious?

CHAPTER TWENTY-SEVEN

Pike's lungs felt like they were going to burst, and yet he pushed on. Three lives depended on him, so he couldn't afford to give in to the pain he felt in his limbs, and his chest, the stitch he felt in his side. His feet seemed to have swelled in size and increased in weight. They were almost impossible to lift, and yet he kept on, stumbling several times, but always righting himself, never allowing himself to fall, because he knew that if he *did* fall he might never get up, and then what would happen to McConnell, and Bright Deer, and poor exhausted Betsy? They would all die, that's what would happen to them, and it would be his fault. He didn't want to have to live with that on his conscience, knowing that three people had died—his *best friend*—all because he couldn't put one foot in front of the other, anymore. . . .

"Hold up," Forester said.

"What is it?" Billings asked.

They all stopped, and Forester raised a hand for silence.

"I thought I . . . heard something," he said, listening intently.

And then Billings heard it, and the others. Someone was coming towards them, on foot, and it wasn't so much that they could hear his footsteps. They were actually able to hear him *talking*.

It sounded like he was saying things like, "One foot in front of the other . . . come on, damn it . . . left, right, left, right . . ." over and over again, a chant, a litany of some sort . . . and then there he was, right in front of them . . .

"Pike!" Forester said, recognizing the man.

Pike, however, did not see the eleven men sitting on horseback, and would have run right past them if Forester and Billings hadn't dropped down off their horses and stopped him.

"No," Pike said to them, trying to get away, "have to keep going . . . keep running . . . get help . . ."

"Pike," Forester said, taking the big man by the shoulders, "we're here, help is here. It's Lee Forester, Pike. Do you know me?"

Pike stopped struggling, and stopped talking. He narrowed his eyes, staring at Forester intently.

"Forester?" he asked.

"That's right," Forester said. "Lee Forester." Over his shoulder he said to Billings, "Water, quickly."

Billings hurriedly retrieved his water bag and handed it to Forester.

"Here," Forester said, handing it to Pike, "take some . . . but not a lot . . ."

Pike took the bag of water, but before sipping it he slid to his knees. Forester held him tightly, easing him down to the ground, until he was sitting. Only then did Pike take a few sips of water.

"Pike," Forester said, "who else survived? Who else is out there?"

Pike looked at Forester, and then thrust the water bag away from him.

"McConnell," he said. "Skins is out there."

"And who else?"

"Women," Pike said. "Betsy Walters . . . Bright Deer . . ."

"Anyone else, Pike?"

"No," Pike said, "no one else. We have to help them. Dark Moon . . . the Blackfeet . . ."

"We have to get you back to camp, Pike," Forester said. "I'll have two men take you back, and the rest of us will move on."

"No," Pike said, his breathing beginning to slow, to regulate, "no, I promised I'd be back . . . and I'm going to keep my promise."

"Pike—"

"Let's not waste time arguing," Pike said.

Forester studied Pike for a few moments, and realized there would be no *point* in arguing.

"All right," Forester said, "you can ride double with me. Can you get up?"

"I'll get up," Pike said. "I'll get up . . . help me up, damn it."

Dying just didn't sit well with him. Even if he could pick off Dark Moon, it certainly wouldn't compensate for being killed a moment later. Besides, Pike had to be given a fighting chance to bring back help. McConnell knew the only way Pike wouldn't return was if he was dead, and since the Blackfeet were behind them and not ahead of them, that didn't seem probable, unless Pike simply dropped dead from exhaustion.

McConnell found a high point from which he could watch their back trail, and after about half an hour he squinted to make sure he was seeing correctly—and he was. He could make out a large group of men on horseback, and after a few moments it became clear that it was the Blackfeet.

He hurried back to the clearing in which he had left Bright Deer and Betsy.

Bright Deer's excellent hearing picked up McConnell's return well before the man came into view.

"We have to move," he said, crouching down next to her and Betsy. "They're comin'."

"She cannot move," Bright Deer said.

"Here," McConnell said, "you carry my rifle, and whatever supplies you can handle. Whatever you can't carry, hide."

"And you?"

He slid his hands beneath Betsy's supine form and said, "I'll carry her."

"You can't—" Bright Deer started, but McConnell ignored her, took Betsy into his arms and stood up.

Bright Deer studied him for a few seconds, then stood up and gathered whatever she could carry.

"Which way?" she asked.

"There," McConnell said. He turned and used Betsy's feet to point the way. "We'll try to hide and see if they bypass us."

Bright Deer frowned and said, "If that happens, they might catch up to Pike."

"Let's hope Pike reaches help before that happens," McConnell said. "If we can get them to pass us, we might be safe for awhile. We could all use the rest—especially Betsy."

Bright Deer looked doubtful. At this point she doubted that a few hours' rest would be enough for Betsy to recover her strength.

McConnell, too, knew that wasn't the case. Betsy needed days of rest and proper nutrition before she would regain her strength, but all he could offer her at the moment was a few hours . . . hopefully.

They moved away from the clearing and continued to walk, even though McConnell's legs felt as if there was no strength left in them. Bright Deer took the lead, and McConnell tried to ignore the physical strain carrying Betsy's dead weight was putting on him. He was a strong man, but in his present condition, she felt as if she weighed as much as a grizzly.

"Wait . . ." Bright Deer said presently, and McConnell stopped, stood still and waited while she went on ahead.

After a few minutes she returned, looking excited about something.

"I found a cave," she said.

"A cave?"

She nodded, and said, "This way."

He followed, feeling some renewed strength. A cave would have been too much to hope for. It would offer a hiding place from the Blackfeet, and shelter from the weather. In a cave they'd be able to build a fire without fear of signalling their position to the Blackfeet. The warmth of the fire would be good for Betsy—not to mention him and Bright Deer, as well. It would make them more comfortable while they waited to die.

"There," she said, pointing.

The mouth of the cave was fairly obvious, but there was a chance that the Blackfeet would not come this way. If they did, there was no way they could miss seeing it, but if they *didn't* pass by. . . .

He could see that Bright Deer was thinking the same thing.

"It looks like our only chance," McConnell said. "Let's take it."

Bright Deer nodded, and led the way to the mouth of the cave.

CHAPTER TWENTY-EIGHT

"Pike," Forester said at one point, are you sure we're goin' the right way?"

"I'm positive."

"You know, you were sort of out of it when we found you," Forester said. "Who knows how far off the path you had drifted . . ."

"I didn't drift," Pike said. "If we keep going in this direction, we'll run into them."

"Or into the Blackfeet," Forester said.

"That's possible," Pike said, "but we've got enough men to give them a tussle."

"Well, I'd rather just find McConnell and the women and get back to camp, where we have *more* than enough men," Forester said.

"Agreed," Pike said.

Pike wished he had his own horse to ride. He felt out of place and disoriented riding behind Forester this way, like just so much excess baggage.

He wouldn't admit it to Forester, but he was starting to worry that perhaps he *might* have drifted off course a bit. They should have found McConnell and the women by now, unless McConnell had decided to move them.

Earlier, Forester had sent Billings out ahead of them to act as a scout. Now he saw Billings riding back towards them, and called a halt to their progress.

"What is it?" Forester said.

"Blackfeet," Billings said. "From the size of the party, I'd say they have to be the ones Pike's talkin' about."

"How far ahead?" Forester asked.

"Half an hour, maybe, if we both keep movin' towards each other," Billings said.

"No sign of McConnell and the women?" Pike asked.

Billings looked at Pike and said, "I didn't see them, but I found this," From behind him he produced a water bag, more empty than filled, and showed it to Pike.

"That's McConnell's," Pike said. "Where was it?"

"From the looks of it, they hid it," Billings said. "I found it by accident."

Abruptly, Pike dropped down from behind Forester and took the bag from Billings.

"That means they've moved," Pike said, "possibly to hide. They have to be hidden somewhere between us and the Blackfeet."

"What do you suggest?" Forester asked. "Keep movin' or wait?"

"I'll keep movin'," Pike said. "You and your men

230

spread out and wait. If the Blackfeet get this far, your best bet is to ambush them."

"And you?"

"I'll try and find McConnell and the women," Pike said.

"I'll give you a horse—" Forester started, but Pike cut him off.

"No, I'll go on foot," Pike said. "The Blackfeet might hear me if I go on horseback."

"Pike," Forester said, "you're exhausted. Let me send someone else."

"I'll go," Billings offered.

"Thanks to both of you," Pike said, "but this is my responsibility."

Forester regarded Pike for a few moments, then nodded shortly.

"All right," he said. "Here, take this." He handed Pike his Kentucky pistol, which was much like the one Pike had given to Bright Deer. "You might need the extra firepower."

"Thanks," Pike said. He accepted it and tucked it into his belt.

"If you hear a bunch of rifles bein' fired, you'll know we met up with the Blackfeet," Forester said.

"We'll take care of them for you," Billings said, confidently. "You find your friends."

Pike accepted Billings' hand, then shook hands with Forester and acknowledged the good wishes of the other men, after which he proceeded on foot.

Pike could feel the weakness in his thighs and legs, but he could not afford to give into it. He knew that McConnell and the women had to be nearby, perhaps even within shouting distance. He could not afford to shout, though, not with the Blackfeet approaching.

He just hoped he'd be able to find them before the Blackfeet did.

Inside the cave McConnell waited while Bright Deer spread a blanket over the cold ground before setting Betsy down. His relief was immediate as he laid her down, and he almost felt dizzy as a result of it.

"Are you all right?" Bright Deer asked.

He nodded, but sat down heavily next to Betsy.

"In a minute," he said.

"I will build a fire," she said. "You rest."

McConnell nodded and waved his hand.

He wished the mouth of the cave was smaller, and that there was enough brush nearby that he could use some of it to hide the entrance, but none of that was possible. The mouth of the cave was large and very much within sight of anyone passing close enough. There was just no way to hide it. He was going to have to sit at the mouth with his rifle, and with Pike's Kentucky pistol, which he'd get from Bright Deer. If the Blackfeet found the cave, maybe he'd be able to hold them off long enough for Pike to arrive with help.

When Bright Deer returned with the makings of a fire, he asked her for the pistol. When she asked why, he explained, and she gave it to him. She had no doubt that he'd be more accurate with it than she was.

"I will reload for you," she said, "when the time comes."

Privately, McConnell had some doubts about whether or not they'd even have the time to reload. If the Blackfeet rushed them and were not put off by the first two shots, he'd never have a chance to fire again.

He didn't tell her that, though. Instead he said, Good, that'll help."

Pike moved slowly but surely on foot. He didn't hurry, because he didn't want to make too much noise, and he also didn't want to wear himself out too soon. He knew how weak he was, and if he pushed too hard he wouldn't be any good to anyone.

He walked among the rocks and brush, staying away from the route he would have taken if he'd been on horseback. Where he was walking, there wasn't any room for a horse to move.

McConnell had probably decided that waiting out in the open to die was the wrong move. Knowing McConnell as he did, he knew his friend wouldn't accept death with open arms, even if he was surrounded by a band of Blackfeet warriors.

With Betsy unable to move, they would have looked for shelter somewhere near the spot where Pike had left them. Pike hoped he could get to that spot before the Blackfeet did, and then track McConnell and the women to their shelter. If the Indians got there first—and if they didn't bypass the spot—they might track his friends down, instead.

It was probably McConnell's hope that the Blackfeet would miss them and keep on going. That was Pike's wish, too. If that happened, the Blackfeet would run smack into an ambush. Most of them would end up dead, and the others would scatter. Hopefully, that would be the end of this little adventure. Pike, McConnell, Betsy, and Bright Deer would be able to go to Nathan Wynan's camp, get some rest, and then get on with their lives.

This Blackfoot brave, Dark Moon, was stubborn. Pike would like to have met him now, and maybe even kill him. Then he wouldn't have to look forward to running into him again in the future—because that's what would happen. If Dark Moon got away, he and Pike would encounter each other again, maybe at a time when Dark Moon was a full chief.

Either that, or Dark Moon's own people would kill him before he could rise to that level. Since the initial attack on Joe Gall's camp, nothing had gone quite right for anyone—including Dark Moon. The brave's only redemption would be to bring Pike's hair back to his people—and Pike didn't intend that to happen.

Forester had told Pike that Gall had died, and

Pike was sorry. The man was no leader, but no one deserved to freeze to death the way he did, losing pieces of himself first.

He shuddered, and hoped he'd find McConnell and the women before the same thing happened to them.

The inside of the cave was warm. McConnell could tell *how* warm because he was sitting by the entrance. The warmth was hitting his back, while the cold air came in and struck him in the face. Still, it was nice to be able to feel the warmth, and to have the fire without the danger of it being seen. Of course, the Blackfeet might *smell* it, but that was a chance he was willing to take. The fire might be just the thing to keep Betsy alive until Pike returned.

Of course, McConnell could admit to himself the possibility that Pike *wouldn't* return, but knowing his friend he felt *almost* certain that he *would* return.

The question was, of course, would he return in time?

CHAPTER TWENTY-NINE

When Pike reached the clearing where he had left McConnell and the women, he could see that he had arrived before the Blackfeet. There was no sign that a band of Indian ponies had trod there. There was also no sign of the pony he had left behind with them.

He looked around and found where McConnell and the others had hidden whatever supplies they had been unable to carry with them. Obviously, McConnell had been carrying Betsy, so that Bright Deer had to take whatever she could carry.

Suddenly, Pike became aware of the approach of horses. From the sound, they were unshod ponies, which indicated that the Blackfeet had finally caught up.

Hurriedly, he studied the ground for any sign of which way McConnell and the women had gone. McConnell, however, had been careful *not* to leave any obvious sign. Therefore, Pike was forced to rely upon his own instinct.

Which way would *he* have gone, if he had been in McConnell's place?

Hastily, he made his choice and moved away from the clearing.

Dark Moon raised his hand to call a stop to their progress. They were in a clearing, and the Blackfoot brave studied the ground. Because of Pike's reputation—his status as a "legend" to those who lived in the mountains—he knew that the man might have been there and not left any obvious trace.

Behind him his braves were restless. They were eager to be on their way, to continue to run to ground the whites. Dark Moon knew that many of his braves were now thinking of returning home.

"Dark Moon—" one of the braves said, but he fell silent when his leader turned his head to look at him.

Dark Moon turned, then, to look behind him. Counting himself, he had twenty men with him, out of the forty he had originally started with.

"Black Dog," Dark Moon said, addressing the brave next to him.

"Yes?"

"You will take fifteen braves with you and continue on," Dark Moon said.

"Fifteen?"

"I will take the other four," Dark Moon said, "and look around here. We will catch up to you."

Black Dog didn't quite understand what Dark Moon had in mind, but it was not his place to question his leader's instructions.

Dark Moon took a moment to choose the four braves he would keep with him, and then Black Dog and the others moved out.

Dark Moon turned and looked at the four braves he had chosen to stay with him.

"We will look around," he said.

"What are we looking for, Dark Moon?" one of them asked.

Dark Moon said, "I am not sure. I just have a . . . a feeling . . ."

"Should we separate," the brave asked, "and spread out?"

"No," Dark Moon said, "we will stay together. Follow me."

Pike, moving away from the clearing, could hear the riders stop. He, then, also stopped and stood stock still, not wanting to be heard. He could hear voices, but could not hear what was being said. When the horses began moving once again, he quietly started walking. He felt, however, that he wasn't hearing *all* of the horses ride away. If McConnell had hoped that by hiding, the Blackfeet would pass them by, it seemed that his plan had only partially worked.

Pike continued at a faster pace, not knowing how many of the Blackfeet braves might now be coming in the same direction.

* * *

McConnell felt sleepy. He was afraid that the warmth of the fire might be lulling him to sleep. He turned, and saw that Bright Deer had fallen asleep next to the already sleeping Betsy Walters. If *he* fell asleep . . .

Suddenly he heard something, and turned his head sharply. All traces of the desire to sleep were now gone. He left the rifle on the ground next to him, and raised the pistol in his hand.

"What is it?" Bright Deer asked from directly behind him.

He hadn't heard her approach.

"Someone's comin'," he said.

"Who?"

I suppose we'll have to wait and see."

Pike was now sure that there were some Blackfeet warriors on his heels. If they weren't tracking him, they were certainly moving in the same direction. Suddenly, he saw the entrance to a cave ahead of him and knew, even before he saw McConnell, that his friends would be inside.

"It is Pike," Bright Deer said. McConnell was surprised at the emotion in her voice. There were several possible reasons he could think of, but what ever the reason was, she was clearly very pleased to see Pike.

"Stay here," McConnell said.

He stepped outside just enough for Pike to see him. The bigger man waved, and hurried over.

"We found this cave," McConnell said. "Actually, Bright Deer found it. It seemed better than just waiting out in the open."

"Let's go inside," Pike said. "I'm sure there are some Blackfeet behind me."

"Dark Moon and his men?"

Pike waited until they were inside to answer. As they entered the cave, the warmth of the fire enveloped him.

"Pike," Bright Deer said.

Pike smiled at her, then looked over at Betsy, lying on the floor with a blanket over her.

"How is she?" he asked.

"Not good," Bright Deer said.

Pike looked at McConnell. "I think the Blackfeet have split into two groups. One, the major group, moved on. The other, I feel, was just behind me."

"Looking for us," McConnell said, "just in case *we* also split up."

"Which we did," Bright Deer said.

"Yes," Pike said, "but now we're back together."

"Just in time," McConnell said.

Bright Deer frowned and said, "In time for what?"

Pike looked at her, then at McConnell and said, "That's what we're going to find out, I guess."

* * *

After Pike left them, Forester had his men dismount and spread out. Two men took all of the horses back about a hundred yards and stood by them. The rest of the men, armed with rifles, sought positions from which they could mount an effective ambush.

Forester and Billings took up a position together.

"What do you think?" Billings asked.

"About what?"

Billings shrugged.

"About ambushing these Blackfeet."

"I don't have a problem with it," Forester said. "They're savages, and they've already killed most — if not all — of Joe Gall's men. This is no more than what they deserve."

"Maybe," Billings said, "it just seems sort of . . . cowardly to me."

Forester gave the man a sharp look.

"Oh, don't worry," Billings said, "when the time comes, I'll do my part — I just won't like it."

Forester's sharp look gave way to a smile, and he said, "I'd worry about you if you did."

CHAPTER THIRTY

With the arrival of Pike in the cave, their fire-power suddenly doubled. Once again, Bright Deer was given Pike's Kentucky pistol.

Pike and McConnell spent some time putting together a hasty plan, and then Pike spoke to Bright Deer.

"Sit by Betsy, Bright Deer," Pike said.

"I want to help," she said.

"You will be," Pike said, "by staying by Betsy. If she wakes up she might call out, or scream, and give us away before we *want* to be given away."

"All right," she said, accepting his explanation.

"Bright Deer," he said, then, "Skins and I are going to go outside and wait. We don't think it's in our best interests to be trapped in here when the Blackfeet come."

"I will be trapped in here," she pointed out.

"Hopefully," he said, "by us being outside, we'll be able to keep that from happening. I'm convinced that most of the Blackfeet kept going, figuring to run us down. Instead, they're going to run into some of Nathan Wynan's men, who will be more than prepared for them."

"Pike and I are gonna go outside and prepare for the rest of them," McConnell said.

"Hopefully," Pike said, "this will be over very shortly."

To himself he added, one way or another.

"I trust you," she said. "I will wait here."

"Don't trust me too much," Pike said. "Keep that pistol at hand."

"I will."

"Let's go," Pike said to McConnell, "before we *do* get trapped in here."

They hurried out of the cave entrance and looked around.

"I'll go over there," Pike said, pointing to a cluster of rocks.

McConnell had noticed a ledge above the cave entrance earlier.

"I'll go up there," he said. "With you over there, we'll almost have them in a crossfire."

"Good," Pike said. "We should be able to surprise them."

"How many do you figure we'll have to deal with?" McConnell asked.

"I didn't *see* them split up, Skins," Pike said. "From the way it sounded, I'd say half a dozen or so stayed behind."

"Six," McConnell said, rubbing his jaw thoughtfully. "That doesn't sound too bad."

"Let's get into position," Pike said. "Let's end this thing once and for all."

"I'm for that," McConnell said. "Think about where you want to sit and fish, because that's all I'm looking forward to after all of this."

"I know just the place," Pike said.

"Where?"

Pike patted his friend on the shoulder and said, "I'll tell you if we live through this."

Forester had placed one man well ahead of the rest of them, and when he turned and waved, he said to Billings, "Here they come."

Billings turned and said, "Get ready," to someone, who then passed it on to the others.

"Remember," Forester said, loud enough for all to hear him, "nobody fires until I do."

It would only take one nervous shot to alert the Blackfeet of the ambush, and then they'd lose them, giving them a chance to regroup.

"Nice and easy, Forester said to himself. "Let's get them the first time out."

Pike and McConnell took up position just in time. They had only gotten settled when two Blackfeet braves came into view, on foot. They were sitting ducks, but Pike knew that there were others about, maybe even Dark Moon. To kill these two — easy prey that they were — would only serve to alert the others.

He knew that, and he knew that McConnell was aware of it, as well.

The two braves were walking gingerly, studying the ground. If they would only look up they would see the entrance to the cave. When that happened, one of two things would occur. They would either go and investigate it together, or they would go and get the other braves and show it to them.

If these two chose to investigate on their own, Pike and McConnell would have to kill them in order to protect Bright Deer and Betsy. Pike would have preferred that the braves play it cautious, and go for the others before they investigated.

He looked up and saw McConnell looking over at him. He placed his index finger to his lips, trying to relay to McConnell that if they had to kill these two, they had to do it quietly. McConnell nodded and emulated his movement, indicating that he understood.

Now they could only wait and see what these two braves would decide to do.

Forester felt the tension in his shoulders, and knew that his men felt it, as well.

Finally, they were able to see the Blackfeet. As they came into view, Forester counted. There were fifteen of them, and while they outnumbered him and his men by several, the element of surprise would more than even up the odds. It would actually give them the advantage.

He raised his rifle and sighted down the barrel,

but was determined to wait until the Indians got much closer to them. He wanted the first volley of shots to be as effective as possible.

Dark Moon studied the ground and knew that he and his braves were going to find somebody. The whites had split up; he only hoped that the man *they* would find would be Pike, and not the other.

Dark Moon could have gone on with the bulk of his men instead of staying behind, and he did not quite know why he had chosen not to. Perhaps he had made his decision through some sort of instinct. Perhaps he *felt* that Pike was somewhere in the area.

Perhaps he felt that, finally, the hunt was going to end.

Pike watched as one of the braves looked up from the ground. He could tell from the expression on the man's face that he had seen the entrance to the cave. He went over to the other brave and called his attention to it, and then the two braves put their heads together to discuss the matter. If they made a move towards the cave, Pike and McConnell were going to have to make a move of their own—but quietly. Pike decided that if the braves started for the cave, he was going to rush them. He might possibly surprise them enough to freeze them just long enough for him to reach them.

The two braves had what seemed to be a long conversation about the situation — although it was only a few moments — and then they turned and walked away, out of sight.

Obviously, they were going to call the others. Pike hoped that when they returned their leader, Dark Moon, would be with them.

CHAPTER THIRTY-ONE

Forester sighted down the barrel of his rifle at the lead brave, wondering if this was the leader. He was riding in the lead, though, so this was the first brave who was going to get shot.

"Three . . . two . . . one . . ." he said, and pulled the trigger.

After that, the shots were impossible to count. . . .

The two braves returned, with three others. Although Pike had never gotten a close look at Dark Moon, he felt sure that this was him. He was the tallest of the braves, and they walked in deference to him, making it obvious that he was their leader.

The two braves who had found the cave pointed to it and spoke to Dark Moon. Dark Moon was speaking to them when they all heard the first shot . . . and the volleys that followed. . . .

Dark Moon looked up, and listened. Pike was afraid that all five of them would run away, and it seemed as if they would, but then Dark Moon spoke sharply, and the other four braves froze in place.

Pike looked up at McConnell, and saw that he was aiming his rifle. Pike raised his rifle to his shoulder, and it occurred to him that he and McConnell might *both* be aiming at Dark Moon. That would be a waste of one of their shots. At the last moment he moved the barrel of his rifle and shot the brave standing on Dark Moon's right just as McConnell shot the brave standing on Dark Moon's left.

"Shit!" Pike said.

The first volley from Forester and his men dropped seven Blackfeet braves from their ponies to the ground. The others fought to control their ponies and looked around in confusion. By the time they were able to turn their ponies, some of the men — including Forester — had reloaded. They aimed and fired again, and four more braves were snatched from their ponies' backs. That left four braves who turned their animals and started to run.

"Mount up," Forester shouted. "We'll go after them." He turned to Billings and said, "Tate, keep two men and check to make sure that the others are all dead."

"Right."

Forester ran for his horse, mounted up, and led most of his men after the fleeing braves.

* * *

As the braves to his right and left fell, Dark Moon reacted instantly. He turned and ran. The other two braves with him seemed undecided about what to do. One of them died a moment later when Bright Deer came out of the cave and fired Pike's Kentucky pistol.

Pike broke from cover and ran after Dark Moon.

McConnell dropped down from his ledge and went after the other brave, who had also decided to flee.

He shouted at Bright Deer, "Stay with Betsy!", and she nodded and went back inside the cave.

As Pike ran after Dark Moon, he felt his legs betraying him. Rather than running, he was staggering. He could see Dark Moon ahead of him, and the Blackfoot leader was running very fast. Pike took the pistol Forester had given him from his belt, aimed at the fleeing brave, and fired. He saw Dark Moon stagger as the ball hit him, but the man kept on running. Pike, feeling as if his lungs were on fire, came to a halt and fell to his knees.

McConnell would never have caught his brave, except for the fact that Forester and his men had chased their four braves back to this point, as well. In fact, the brave McConnell was chasing was almost trampled by his own fleeing brothers, and then Forester and his men were on them, firing. McConnell had not had time to reload, so he simply stopped running and dropped to the ground to catch his breath. He watched as the four mounted braves, and the one he was chasing, were shot and killed by Forester and his men.

He wondered where Pike was. . . .

As the ball struck Dark Moon in the side, pain lanced through him, but he kept running. He had to reach his pony and get away. When he got back to his camp there would be no shame in telling his chief that he and his men were attacked by the legend, He-Whose-Head-Touches-the-Sky. He would say that the legend was true, and that Pike could not be killed. He would also say that when his wound healed, he would go after Pike, anyway, and kill him.

He knew that he would either be hailed as a hero—or he would be killed as a coward. He felt that the first would happen, since he was the chief's son, and the apple of his father's eye.

Pike wearily picked himself up off the ground and walked slowly back to the cave. When he got there, he saw McConnell, Forester and a couple of other men had already reached there.

"Dark Moon?" McConnell said.

"He got away," Pike said, "but he's carrying a piece of lead. The others?"

"All dead," Forester said.

"All of them?"

Forester nodded.

Pike looked at McConnell and said, "So it's over."

"For now," McConnell said.

Pike said, "Dark Moon will have a lot of explaining to do. It may take him a while."

"You had some women with you," Forester said.

"In the cave," Pike said. "One of them needs medical attention pretty bad."

"We'll get them back to camp," Forester said. "We'll get you all back to camp, where you can get some well deserved rest."

Pike looked at McConnell, who was smiling, and said, "Sounds good to me."

Two weeks later Pike awoke with Bright Deer straddling him.

"No," he said.

"Yes," she said.

"I'm tired."

"Yes," she said, again.

"You're selfish," he said.

And she said, "Yes," again. . . .

They had been sleeping together in this tent since their arrival in Nate Wynan's camp. They both knew that today was the day he and McConnell would be leaving. It had already been decided that she and Betsy would be staying with Wynan's camp.

She leaned over now, dangling her full breasts in his face. He licked her nipples, then pulled them into his mouth and sucked them each in turn. She reached between them to hold his rigid penis, then lifted her hips and brought herself down on him, taking him inside. She rode him that way. She enjoyed being on top, and he wanted her to enjoy herself — especially now, since this was the last time they would be together.

Later, Pike came out of the tent and found McConnell waiting with the horses Wynan had given them. Wynan had also given them supplies, and a mule to carry them.

"You look worn out," McConnell said.

"So do you."

"Sayin' goodbye is hard," McConnell said, with a grin.

He handed Pike the reins of his horse as Wynan came walking over.

"You know, you fellas are welcome to stay longer," the man said.

"We know," Pike said.

"And we appreciate the offer," McConnell said.

"But we've got some fishing to do," Pike said.

"We're just gonna take it easy for a while."

"A long while," Pike said.

"Can't say I blame you for that," Wynan said, "after what you fellas went through."

He shook hands with both men, who then mounted up and rode out of camp.

They rode in silence for a good two hours and then McConnell said, "Pike?"

"Yeah?"

"Next time we see smoke from somebody's fire?"

"Yeah."

"Remind me to ride the other way?"

Pike looked at his friend and said, "You can bet on it."